Reflect

Also by

P. N. FURBANK

SAMUEL BUTLER (1835-1902)

ITALO SVEVO: THE MAN AND THE WRITER

REFLECTIONS ON THE WORD 'IMAGE'

P. N. FURBANK

Secker & Warburg
LONDON

First published in England 1970 by
Martin Secker & Warburg Limited
14 Carlisle Street, London W1

SBN 436 16852 9

Printed in Great Britain by
C. Tinling & Co. Ltd,
London and Prescot

CONTENTS

ACKNOWLEDGEMENTS

The author and publishers would like to thank the following for their permission to quote from copyright material: Philip Larkin for 'High Windows'; Fulcrum Press for 'A Walk' from *A Range of Poems*, copyright © Gary Snyder 1966; New Directions Publishing Company Inc. and MacGibbon & Kee Limited for 'Poem' and 'The Pot of Flowers' from *The Collected Earlier Poems*, copyright © 1938 by William Carlos Williams; Faber and Faber Limited and Harper & Row, Publishers, Inc. for 'Out' from *Wodwo* by Ted Hughes.

I would like to thank Graham Martin and Derwent May for suggesting major revisions to the book, and Elizabeth Ellem for correcting the style.

P. N. Furbank

1

DO WE NEED THE TERMS 'IMAGE' AND 'IMAGERY'?

I

It happens every now and then to most people, I think, when they are reading literary criticism, to be puzzled by the words 'image' and 'imagery'. A doubt flits across their mind at reading the words—though rather naturally they ignore it. However, it comes back. And perhaps sometime someone ought to face it, even at the risk of pedantry. That is what I mean to do in this book.

The doubt, of course, is that if you use the word 'image' as a synonym for 'metaphor'—that is to say, to signify a comparison—it is hard to see how this squares with the natural sense of the word 'image', as meaning a likeness, a picture, or a simulacrum. For, after all, a comparison is not a picture. If you read Milton's phrase 'a Forest huge of Spears', the final result of your reading can't be a picture, since you cannot permanently present something to your mind's eye as being both a forest and spears. There is something fundamentally awkward and strange in using the word 'image' as a substitute for 'metaphor' in this way. For the word 'image', unlike 'metaphor', seems to suggest that the end result of what the author is doing is a picture. But what is it a picture of? Which bit of the comparison are you meant to visualise? Or are you meant to visualise both? And if so, how? Successively? Or one on top of the other? Or combined to make a sort of hybrid or monster? Once you start thinking about it, the problem swells and begins to look insuperable.

Since no one would deny that painters and sculptors are concerned with producing 'images' (or have been till very recently) we might begin by thinking about painting. Here things are quite different. In painting you can put on the canvas something—a coloured shape—which can be interpreted equally as spears or a forest; just as in real life you might see a bush which you mistook for a bear. But when it comes to writing, your meaning cannot be indeterminate like this. The word 'spears' means indisputably what it says, there being no feat of skill involved in using the *word* 'spears' as there is in painting spears. You don't have to know how to draw or to use paint and canvas to convey a meaning by it; all you need to do is to write it down.

Of course, a word may be indeterminate in its meaning through being used in two senses simultaneously—for instance in the case of a pun or portmanteau word, as when Pope writes

> Where Bentley late tempestuous wont to sport
> In troubled waters, but now sleeps in Port.

or as when Joyce says that they laid out Finnegan with 'a barrowload of guenesis hoer his head'. But what happens in such a case is quite different from what takes place in painting. For with a pun or a portmanteau word both senses are fully realised (port the drink and port meaning 'harbour'; Guinness and Genesis). Whereas in painting, if a patch of paint can be read both as spears and a forest, it can only be a fairly vague rendering of either—if it were complete, it would be finally identifiable as one or the other.

In painting you can indeed—as Uccello does—present both spears and a forest in different bits of the same painting, thus presenting a visual analogy. And this would have some vague resemblance to a simile in writing. But when people speak of 'images' in writing in the sense of 'comparisons', they are more often than not thinking of metaphors rather than similes. They have in mind the case of a single word or phrase which does duty for two heterogeneous things at the same time—'a *Forest* huge of Spears'; 'who *spaniell'd* him at heels'. The nearest you can get to a metaphor of this kind in painting is what Robert Campin does in his 'Virgin of the Firescreen', in the National Gallery. The firescreen is indisputably a firescreen, but it also suggests a halo. Similarly, religious paintings often, unobtrusively, give common objects the form of the Cross. But these are trivial devices, which we call 'literary' in a slightly disparaging sense. They are not really like metaphor, having none of the rich potentiality of metaphor. For this richness lies in the possibility of two substantial orders of creation, with their own full range of association, being held in conjunction. In 'The Virgin of the Firescreen' only one substantial object is involved—the firescreen—the other half of the comparison (the halo) being merely symbolic and schematic—a sign, not a substantial thing. And the spectator's reaction to these devices is accordingly superficial; it is merely a pleasure at seeing such a trick brought off, as in deciphering an allegory. And it is worth noticing that they work the other way round from metaphor, in that in the case of the painting you are given the real object (the firescreen) and are meant to infer the one it is being likened to (which, by the way, has to be an obvious one, or the analogy would not be practicable). Whereas in a metaphor you are usually first given the thing with which an analogy is being made (the Forest), from which you are to infer the thing which is literally intended (the Spears). You would say, if you were describing 'The Virgin of the Firescreen' in words, that the screen 'haloes' the Virgin's head—from which the reader would infer that it was disc-shaped.

There are also the analogies exploited in *collage*, in which the artist borrows an already existing object, or an already existing photograph or painting of an object, and makes it do duty for something quite different which it happens to resemble: for instance Picasso's sculpture 'Ape with Young', in which the ape's head is made out of two motor-cars. But here again it is precisely because the resemblance—however close or far-fetched—has to be established in a definite single manner (it being in the nature of the plastic arts that they have to commit themselves to one set of lines and planes) that it cannot have the richness of metaphor. For by contrast there is no one right of way of 'realising' a metaphor: there are a hundred ways, and the mind is set to work ranging among them. A sculpture like Picasso's 'Ape with Young' is really more like a pun than a metaphor; it depends on its shock-tactics, and you enjoy it, too, like a wonderful trick.

Of course, I don't mean to deny that there are effects of indeterminacy or multiple meaning in painting which are more than trivial, and contain no trick. Think for instance of the expression on one of the soldiers' faces in Bosch's 'Christ Mocked (The Crowning with Thorns)' in the National Gallery: it is a ferocity with a strange resemblance to tenderness.

But in these effects there is no uncertainty as to what you are actually seeing. The expression on the soldier's face would have had the same ambiguity in real life—so that there is nothing in it which really resembles metaphor, in which we consider one thing *in terms* of another.

II

Metaphor, then, in any serious sense, is peculiar to literature. And if, as I think is the case, you soon get in a muddle if you substitute the word 'image' for the word 'metaphor', it is partly because the word carries with it irrelevant implications from painting and sculpture. It is as though those who use the word in this way were beginning to take *literally* the ancient and useful cliché (*'ut pictura poesis'* and so on) that poets and dramatists 'paint' or 'draw' things. Though nothing could be more obvious than that they do not, *literally*, do anything at all like painting. For, clearly, a writer has only to write the word 'beechtree'—he need not even call it a 'green' beechtree—for the reader to run up a complete imaginary beechtree for him on his own initiative. If a writer were literally a painter, he would have a soft job.

Still, you might think that the sensible attitude to any puzzle about the words 'image' and 'imagery' would be the one expressed by Caroline Spurgeon in *Shakespeare's Imagery and What It Tells Us*:

> . . . few people would entirely agree as to what constitutes an image, and still fewer as to what constitutes a poetic image.
>
> But as Burke wisely says, 'though no man can draw a stroke between the confines of night and day, yet light and darkness are upon the whole tolerably distinguishable', so I believe, for practical purposes. . . . we all know fairly well what we mean by an image. We know that, roughly speaking, it is . . . the little word-picture used by a poet or prose-writer to illustrate, illuminate and embellish his thought. It is a description or an idea, which by comparison or analogy, stated or understood, with something else, transmits to us, through the emotions and associations it arouses, something of the 'wholeness', the depth and richness of the way the writer views, conceives or has felt what he is telling us.

The image thus gives quality, creates atmosphere and conveys emotion in a way no precise description, however clear and accurate, can possibly do.[1]

To amplify this, she quotes, a few lines further down the same page, a line from *Love's Labour's Lost*, about the young Berowne, whose gaiety, wit and charm are such

That aged ears play truant at his tales . . .

And where, you may ask, is the 'little word-picture'? Is it pedantic to ask this? What is it a picture of? What are we meant to visualise? Caroline Spurgeon goes on:

those two metaphorical words call up a host of associations and emotions, and give us the picture of old grave men beguiled from their serious thoughts or labours by merry chatter of attractive and irresponsible youth, elders tempted from their grooves or their duty by fun and lightheartedness, as a boy is tempted to leave his lessons by the play of sunlight on a summer afternoon.[2]

So now, perhaps, we are getting somewhere. Shakespeare means us to picture a schoolboy in a class-room on a sunny day. Yes, but don't schoolboys ever play truant on grey winter's days? Couldn't he have been wanting to go skating? And come to that, is it one schoolboy or a whole class-full of them? Or maybe a schoolgirl?

If Shakespeare's line is a 'word-picture', a 'word-picture' must be a queer sort of picture—one which, according to the person viewing it, depicts old men—or perhaps very young ones, i.e. schoolboys (or then again perhaps schoolgirls)—and the play of sunlight on a summer's afternoon, or perhaps the spectacle of skaters on a winter's afternoon. And then what about those *ears*?

To be sure, Miss Spurgeon tells us that we mustn't be too literal-minded about the word 'image'. It is not to be thought of merely as something visual. 'I suggest that we divest our minds of the hint the term carries with it of visual image only, and think of it, for the present purpose, as connoting any and every kind of imaginative picture or other experience.' And so, for that matter, we can forget the phrase 'word-picture' too. But if an image isn't necessarily a word-picture, or if it need not be a *picture* at all, isn't 'image' a rather awkward name for it?

I have begun with this particular example of a metaphor because the issues it raises are fairly simple. It is harmless enough to call this metaphor an 'image', just because it is obviously inappropriate. For, since readers of the line are at liberty to think up pretty much what pictures they like, depending on their memory or fancy, or on what element in the comparison they are considering (some may try to get the *ears* in), they can hardly believe that the success of the line depends on their forming any particular picture. Shakespeare could not have been depending on their uncontrolled imaginings. Indeed, some readers of the line will hardly make the effort to picture anything at all, the choice open to them being so large, and the impossibility of any particular picture being finally satisfactory being so plain.

But let us take another of Shakespeare's metaphors, Antony's '. . . the hearts That spaniell'd me at heels'. Here, every reader will and must do some mental picture-making. And because this is so, it is rather natural for him to assume that the particular pictures he summons up have some significance in understanding the lines. Yet a moment's reflection will tell you that this can't be so. For whereas everyone pictures something in reading the lines, no two readers will picture the same thing: some will picture a conqueror with fawning followers, some a master with a spaniel, some a hybrid of the two, and some again will try to bring the *hearts* into the picture. (And this quite apart from the fact that no two people will picture a spaniel or a courtier in the same way.) Again, when the same reader reads the passage on another day, he will imagine it differently. Indeed, at the very moment of reading the passage, his picture will be in a constant state of metamorphosis—mobility being in the nature of mental imagery. Though, further, we must remember that to speak at all of people's mental images as being 'different' or 'the same' is a loose way of talking, since—almost by definition—there is no possibility of directly comparing them. The nearest one can ever get is to ask the people in question to tell us in *words* what they are picturing; and after all, the best words of all for this purpose should really be the ones used by Shakespeare himself.

So, once again, Shakespeare couldn't have been depending on the reader's forming any particular picture, when reading that phrase from *Antony and Cleopatra*. In fact, it is merely a false analogy from painting which makes anyone suppose he did. For consider what an image, in the sense of a picture, is. It is a likeness of something, and a likeness of a particular thing. There may not exist in the real world any particular goldfinch, cage and wall to correspond to the ones in Carel Fabritius's famous painting, but what the beholder of the painting sees is a likeness of something particular, something which is the same for every beholder and which he would recognise if he met it later in real life. Painting works with the particular—a given goldfinch in a given cage occupying a given relationship to the wall behind. Literature works with the general—with words, like 'goldfinch' and 'cage' and 'wall', which stand for classes of things—for all goldfinches, all cages, all walls, however different. If you talk of one painter as having more 'generality' than another (Titian, say, than Monet) you are using a figure of speech—though of course a useful one. And likewise if you talk of one piece of literature being more 'particular' or 'concrete' than another, you are again using a figure of speech. For, strictly speaking, all painting, even non-figurative painting, is particular, and all literature is general.

Even an abstract or non-figurative painting is still *particular*. A blue circle in such a painting is bound to be that particular blue circle and no other; it is not like the words 'blue circle', which apply to all the blue circles that ever were. And on the other hand, though you may speak of a certain type of poetry as being 'intolerably abstract' and prefer a kind which conveys more sense of concrete perception, the distinction is again not to be taken literally. There can be no such thing as Abstract Literature, on the analogy of Abstract Painting, because all literature is abstract, just as all literature is general. There is, indeed, a kind of *avant-garde* writing which has affinities with abstract or non-figurative painting—I mean the kind which makes mainly typographic patterns with words, with only playful and glancing reference to their meaning—but the name given to this is, precisely, Concrete Poetry. And it is only by convenience that it is classed as literature at all, and not as graphic art.

Literature is always general, though with strong yearnings towards the concrete and particular, just as painting is always particular, though with strong yearnings towards the general. Any aspiration towards 'concreteness' on writing's part must be taken no more literally than the baroque architect's ambition to make brick and stone take wing and float. And the same applies to the time-honoured commonplace which describes writers as 'painting' scenes or manners. The phrase merely means that the writer fancies himself in the garb or role of a painter. No poem can be literally a picture or a likeness of anything, like a painting, in the sense that presented with the original you would immediately see that it, and it alone, *was* the original. And one should remember the fact, if it's not too simple to mention, that, if birds do not actually peck at painted cherries, as fable would have us believe, they certainly can be taken in by scarecrows and statues and believe them to be what they represent—just as humans can be deceived by *trompe l'œil* painting. Whereas no-one ever mistook a page of Wordsworth's *Poems* for an old Cumberland beggar. Though one shouldn't lay too much stress on this, because *trompe l'œil* is a freak art-form, and most representational painting works not by practising wholesale deception on the beholder but by stimulating him, under strict control, to deliberate day-dreaming and mental image-formation.

III

But if a picture is a likeness, then an 'image' in the literary sense (or, at least, the sense which makes it a synonym for 'metaphor') can't be a picture. For an 'image' in the sense of a metaphor is not a likeness of anything. True, a metaphor depends on pointing to a likeness between heterogeneous things. But to say that courtiers fawning on a great man resemble spaniels fawning on their master is not saying that spaniels are a *likeness* of fawning courtiers, as Holbein's portrait is a likeness of Henry VIII. There is nothing pictorial about it (though purely as a figure of speech you might say that Shakespeare was 'painting' the courtiers by his vivid metaphor), since the comparison holds for any courtiers and any spaniels. And the fact that you make an effort, drawing on your own store of recollections according to your fancy and degree of involvement, to visualise the comparison in some way or other, doesn't make it any less general and therefore unlike painting.

The truth is that with a poetic metaphor the actual content of readers' mental imagery doesn't matter. And it is a pure example of the 'affective fallacy', the confusion between a poem and its *results*, to think that it does. The author can't control the reader's mental images—the castings-around of the rat in the maze—he merely provides the linguistic maze itself, with its entrance and exit. (He can no more control your mental images than a novelist can control, except within the broadest limits, how you visualise his characters and scenes; otherwise no novel could have more than one illustrator. And as for plays, the way we see deeper into them is precisely by seeing them played on different stages by different actors.) What matters about poetic metaphors is their structure—which is both the logical structure of a process of reasoning, and the architectural structure of words in a line of verse—for that is what the author can control. And just as no two lines of verse have the same rhythm, though they may have the same metre, so no two poetic metaphors have the same structure. What differentiates one metaphor from another is the kind of effort—the length and complexity and particular character of the effort—that trying to 'realise' it demands for the reader. A metaphor is an invitation to an activity, ending in an impossiblity. (For you cannot *actually* think of something in terms of something else: any metaphor must break down somewhere.) It is the activity which matters, an activity which may often be a question, not of forming mental images, but of trying and failing to. When one reads or hears 'Macbeth has murdered Sleep', one tries to realise it in mental pictures but gives up baffled. (This, in fact, worried an eighteenth-century editor, who wanted to amend the line to read 'Macbeth has murdered a sleeper'.) But for all that, it is a very powerful metaphor—since of course that is how it is meant to work, precisely by baffling one's effort to realise it in mental images.

Thus I am not trying to say that, because the mental image-making that a reader goes in for when reading a line of verse is different for each reader, the whole thing is a waste activity. He would be a hopelessly incompetent reader who didn't, on some occasions, make very intense efforts to 'realise' the author's meaning in mental pictures—or who didn't, on other occasions, become conscious of the way in which a particular line or passage tempted him to mental picture-making and then baffled him. All the means by which a reader tries to 'realise' a line of verse, including this one, are important.

For the *kind* of effort he makes—not the content of his effort, but the form of it; and this will never be exactly the same for any two lines of verse—is precisely the thing that the writer can control.

In Milton's lines about Satan's spear:

> His Spear, to equal which the tallest Pine
> Hewn on *Norwegian* hills, to be the Mast
> Of some great Ammiral, were but a wand.

part of the control which Milton exercises over the reader, and of the controlled co-operation which he requires from him, is certainly concerned with visualisation. The reader is encouraged to do some fairly easy mental picturing, before reaching the words 'were but a wand', when he finds that he has been led into a trap; with a jerk, he has to revise his whole image of the pine or mast and consider it as a 'wand'; the effort is too much, and he quickly gives up. The little diagram of effort is the same for every reader, regardless of *how* he actually pictures or combines spear, tree, hills, mast, ship and wand.

Indeed, this is what form in literature is. The essential peculiarity of literature, as compared with the other arts, is that it depends upon a very special kind of 'realisation' on the reader's part. Unlike the spectator of a painting or of architecture, or a listener to music, the reader of literature has to recreate a text in terms of the arbitrary furnishings of his own mind. It is through ignoring this fact that discussions as to whether literary judgement is something 'objective' or merely 'personal' tend not to make much sense. For any reader, in the nature of things, has to take his own route to the 'realisation' of a text and reaches a true reading by a process of convergence.

So I mustn't be understood as echoing Burke, in *On the Sublime and the Beautiful*, where he says that, for the most part, the less poetry tends to 'raise ideas [i.e. mental pictures] of things', the better for it. Burke, who is arguing against the '*ut pictura poesis*' theory, says that in ordinary conversation or reading, words very rarely raise up images in our mind:

> If I say 'I shall go to Italy next summer', I am well understood. Yet I believe nobody has by this painted in his imagination the exact figure of the speaker passing by land or by water, or by both; sometimes on horseback, sometimes

in a carriage; with all the particulars of the journey. Still less has he any idea of Italy, the country to which I proposed to go; or of the greenness of the fields, the ripening of the fruits, and the warmth of the air, with the change to this from a different season, which are the ideas for which the word *summer* is substituted; but least of all has he any image from the word *next*; for this word stands for the idea, of many summers, with the exclusion of all but one: and surely the man who says *next summer*, has no images of such a succession, and such an exclusion.[3]

And where poëtry is concerned, says Burke, this is a good thing.

> . . . so little does poetry depend for its effect on the power of raising sensible images, that I am convinced it would lose a very considerable part of its energy if this were the necessary result of all description. . . . There is not perhaps in the whole *Aeneid* a more grand and laboured passage than the description of Vulcan's cavern in Etna, and the works that are there carried on. Virgil dwells particularly on the formation of the thunder, which he describes unfinished under the hammers of the Cyclops. But what are the principles of this extraordinary composition?
>
> Tres imbris torti radios, tres nubis aquosae
> Addiderant; rutili tres ignis, et alitis austri;
> Fulgores nunc terrificos, sonitumque, metumque
> Miscebant operi, flammisque sequacibus iras.
>
> This seems to me admirably sublime: yet if we attend coolly to the kind of sensible images which a combination of ideas of this sort must form, the chimeras of madmen cannot appear more wild and absurd than such a picture. *Three rays of twisted showers, three of watery clouds, three of fire, and three of the winged south wind; then mixed they in the work terrific lightnings, and sound and fear, and anger, with pursuing flames.* . . . The truth is, if poetry gives us a noble assemblage of words corresponding to many noble ideas, which are connected by circumstances of time or place, or related to each other as cause and effect, or associated in any natural way, they may be moulded together in any form, and perfectly answer their end. The picturesque connection is not demanded, because no real picture is formed . . .[4]

It is an unsympathetic way of talking—particularly that phrase about the 'noble assemblage of words'. It shows up a typical weakness in the Augustan attitude to literature—the tendency to think of literature and art as offering a finished product for the reader's passive delectation or diversion, demanding no effort or co-operation on his part.

However, if one of the ways in which the reader tries to realise an author's metaphors is by visualising, it is far from being the only one. He also realises the metaphor as a pattern of words, following out the ramifications, interaction and ambiguities of their meaning in terms of the dictionary and usage. And it would be an illusion to think there was any real dividing-line between these two kinds of 'realisation'. But then, further, a metaphor is only 'realised' under the control of a particular syntax and sound-sequence and rhythm, which form part of its meaning. A metaphor is not something heterogeneous in the texture of a poem, like a truffle in paté; the words composing it have all sorts of other functions as well —acoustic, rhythmic and associative. It is not *only* a metaphor, any more than a rhyming word is only a rhyme. Nor, indeed, do most people think it is.

They only begin to do so when they use the word 'image' in place of the word 'metaphor'. For the word 'image', with its associations with painting and sculpture and with mental imagery, suggests that the thing it stands for is different from words: that the writer who uses an 'image' is resorting to a non-linguistic means of expression, as a Cubist painter might stick a real newspaper or real mop on his painted canvas. It leads to the belief that you can isolate the 'images' in a work of literature, that you can collect and categorise them and trace patterns in them, so forming a work-within-the-work. And this is a very retrograde step. For the great achievement of modern criticism has been to establish that literary works are integral wholes, and that the various elements composing them only have significance as a part of the whole—so that we now poke fun at the Victorians for collecting gems of wisdom or 'immortal sayings' from Shakespeare. Yet collecting and categorising the 'images' in Shakespeare comes to much the same thing.

IV

The idea at the back of the mind of those who think of metaphors in terms of mental imagery is that a reader's mental images are somehow a copy of the author's meaning. It is a natural mistake to make, because many people still have a false notion of what mental imagery is; though the question has been rather satisfactorily cleared up in the last decade or two, notably by Sartre in *L'Imaginaire* and Gilbert Ryle in *The Concept of Mind.* People still tend to think of mental images as having an actual optical reality,* as if 'seeing' things in the head were fundamentally not different from seeing them in the world outside. They believe that mental pictures are presented to them and that they contemplate them. In fact, as Sartre and Ryle point out, one does not contemplate mental images. A mental image is no less and no more than what you put there. You can never learn anything from mental images, since they are merely a way of presenting to yourself what you already know. It can never happen with a mental image, as it happens all the time when you look at the world outside, that there is something in your field of vision that you can't identify—making you ask yourself, 'is it a bush or a rabbit'? You can never stand back and scrutinise a mental image, since you are fully occupied in creating it—it represents your consciousness in action. If you imagine St. Paul's Cathedral to yourself you cannot *count* the columns of the portico, to see how many there are, for it is entirely up to you how many you put there: '. . . imagining is not only not any sort of observing of anything,' says Ryle, 'it is also not having a sensation of a special sort'. Forming mental pictures is not perceiving or observing a real copy (more or less lifelike) of an external object; it is performing a playful imitation of a man perceiving something. 'A person picturing his nursery . . . is not being a spectator of a resemblance of his nursery, but he is resembling a spectator of his nursery.'

A mental image, as Sartre stresses, has an intrinsic poverty. It has no texture, as the real world has. It is not, like the real world, inexhaustible in its details and the relationships of those details. On the contrary, it is rigidly confined to the few elements and relationships which it immediately offers. Its thinness and

---

* Perhaps the mistake is fostered by the totally different phenomenon of 'after-images' and the flashes that you 'see' when you rub your eyeballs, which of course are a function of the optic nerves.

hollowness is only not apparent because it has a way of papering over its own cracks. A mental image, for instance, may present an object under one aspect, but somehow include a knowledge of all its other aspects (the back as well as the front, etc.), or of other kinds of knowledge about it. This is a familiar experience in dreams, when we 'know' that some rudimentary object, say a fork or the letter 'M', is really a cathedral organ. In the case of waking mental images, however, when the content becomes manifestly too great for the image that is standing for it, we create a new image (images always exist as a whole; one does not add to or subtract from an image, one replaces it by a new one).

A mental image, because of its poverty, can never contain *all* that we are thinking about anything; it is merely an adjunct to thinking about it, often rather loosely tied to our real thoughts and motives. So that we may form a sketchy picture in our mind of a friend, or of St. Paul's Cathedral, though the *appearance* of either is the last thing we are concerned with: we are really wondering whether our friend has finished his novel, or whether the Dean of St. Paul's is a member of Convocation. Mental image-making, which is a marvellously valuable human acquirement, and can be trained and disciplined in all sorts of fruitful ways, is also a habit, and happens casually when we have no need of it.

One always needs to remind oneself of a simple fact about mental images—that they are a make-believe. The person having them is pretending something to himself. This is why they can be such a source of confusion. Discussions about the nature of 'mental images' tend to get heated. One person says that he has the most beautiful, detailed images; he can picture every stain on the face of Big Ben. Another claims, rather drily, that he hardly ever has such things, and can get on very well without them thankyou. A third, with pride, announces that *he* has them in colour. It is like old ladies discussing their illnesses; there is a touch of competition about the whole thing. People imply by their tone that *theirs* is the really right-thinking way to be.

Francis Galton has a very interesting chapter on all this in his *Inquiries into Human Faculty* (1883). He devised a questionnaire about habits of mental visualisation and first submitted it to friends in the scientific world. The initial group of questions invited them to picture their breakfast-table as it had been that morning and then to answer the following queries: 'Is the image dim or fairly clear? Is its brightness comparable to that of the actual scene? Are all the objects well defined at the same time, or is the place of sharpest definition at any one moment more contracted than it is in a real scene? Are the colours of the china, of the toast, bread-crust, mustard, meat, parsley or whatever may have been on the table, quite distinct and natural? The answers took him by surprise. 'To my astonishment I found that the great majority of the men of science to whom I applied protested that mental imagery was unknown to them. He had better luck with people in 'general society', and he eventually arranged the answers of a group of a hundred adult subjects in order of their visualising ability. Their reports ranged from

1. Brilliant, distinct, never blotchy.
2. Quite comparable to the real object. I feel as though I was dazzled, e.g. when recalling the sun to my mental vision.

to

100. My powers are zero. To my consciousness there is no association of memory with objective visual impressions. I recollect the breakfast-table but do not see it.

Among his informants there was also Mr. Flinders Petrie, who told him that 'he habitually works out sums by aid of an imaginary sliding rule, which he sets in the desired way and reads off mentally. He does not usually visualise the whole rule, but only that part of it with which he is at the moment concerned.' And there was an eminent mineralogist who assured him that 'he is able to imagine simultaneously all the sides of a crystal with which he is familiar'.

However, there is a point which escapes all these witnesses; it is that mental images are what you tell yourself that they are. They 'stand in' for what you know should be there. And the difference between a retired general fighting over his battles at the dinner-table with forks and glasses, and his doing it in solitude, 'in his head', is not very great. In conjuring up something in mental imagery you do exactly the amount of making-believe to yourself that you personally require. As long as it allows you to pretend to yourself convincingly: 'You've got Rommel's outfit over there, at six o'clock, behind that bushy-topped palm, and here are our chaps creeping up the *wadi*', or 'I am seeing a woman in a richly brocaded dress', then that's all that's needed. And if you want to pretend to yourself that you are seeing in colour, who is to stop you? No one can contradict you. I mean, they can't say 'no, no, you're *not* pretending to see that dress in colour'.

It is this central fact about 'mental imagery' which makes discussions of 'images' and 'imagery' in their various other senses, and especially their literary sense, so confusing. For in using the words as terms in literary criticism, people usually have the 'mental images' sense somewhere in the back of their mind. And since, in that sense, the words refer to something which does not actually occur, only something which people pretend occurs, their discussions sometimes sound like conversations between madmen.

One of the most interesting suggestions I have read about the relation of mental images to literature occurs in A. D. Nuttall's *Two Concepts of Allegory* (1967). Part of what he has to say is certainly right; and it's significant that when he goes wrong, as I think he does, it is through treating 'mental images' with more respect than they deserve. Nuttall argues that the logical troubles which allegory is alway getting into—such as that Mercy, in order to combat Cruelty, has to resort to very *un*merciful weapons—are very like the bothers that Plato gets into with his 'universals'. It is always a stumbling-block to modern readers that Plato should make Socrates ask whether Beauty is not itself beautiful, or whether Smallness, since it includes many instances of the small, is not larger than them. And indeed, neither allegory nor Plato's handling of universals will stand up to logical scrutiny; yet they are both ways of thought that the mind rests surprisingly comfortably in; and the reason, Nuttall argues, is psychological—it lies in the phenomenon of mental imagery. For one of the peculiarities of mental images is that they seem to be able to combine the particular and the general. Mental images, he says, can be 'non-specific'—that is to say, while remaining a concrete experience, they may represent not just how an object would look on a given occasion to a single observer, but a sort of general and inclusive notion of it, almost like a Platonic Idea.

Many writers have had fun at the expense of this idea of 'non-specified' images. When Locke first suggested that you could form an image of a triangle which was neither equilateral, nor right-angled, nor scalene, but all and none of these at the same time, Berkeley became ribald. He remarked:

> If any man has the faculty of framing in his mind such an idea of a triangle as is here described, it is vain to dispute him out of it, nor would I go about it.[5]

However, Nuttall argues, the testimony quoted in Francis Galton's *Inquiries into Human Faculty* shows, surprisingly, that Locke was right and Berkeley wrong. There is no reason to doubt the word of the 'eminent mineralogist' who told Galton that he was 'able to imagine simultaneously all the sides of a crystal with which he is familiar'. And if it is possible to form an image of an object *in general* in this way—an image which is both the *concept* 'crystal' and an instance of it—then it becomes easier to see where Plato came by his Smallness which is itself small.

It is a beautiful and convincing explanation. But of course it does not depend on anyone ever having had such a thing as a 'non-specified' image, only on people believing they did. However, Nuttall seriously holds that such things occur. And I find this strange. I think it shows how easily credulity slips in, when it comes to this question of mental images. Nuttall, indeed, draws the line himself when E. B. Titchener (another contributor to the debate about 'non-specified' images) claims he can even manage Locke's famous triangle.

> It is a flashy thing, come and gone from moment to moment: it hints two or three red angles, with the red lines deepening into black, seen on a dark green ground. It is not there long enough for me to say whether the angles join to form the complete figure, or even whether all three of the necessary angles are given. Nevertheless it means triangle . . .

Nuttall has to point out that this pretty piece of fireworks is a long way from being 'just triangle'.

> It is 'red and black triangle', 'flashing triangle'—and in both of these descriptions it is the word 'triangle' which is the less appropriate description of the idea as a phenomenon, for

> Titchener admits that he is not certain how many angles it has. He is forced to say of his 'non-specified' image what he says of his definite image—that it *means* triangle. And . . . *anything* can be made to *mean* triangle.[6]

But, after all, surely that is the case against the whole idea of 'non-specific' images? Mental images being make-believe anyway, what is there to stop you telling yourself you can imagine a triangle-in-general—or anything else for that matter? As long as you summon up *something*, some 'flashy' spectrum or other which seems to have to do with triangles or crystals, the will-to-believe will do the rest. Knowing that the thing means 'triangle-in-general' or 'crystal-in-general' you happily tell yourself that it not only means it but is it.

Berkeley was right, and even Nuttall's gingerly gesture towards 'non-specified' images is too much against common sense. And I think it leads him into further fallacies. For he asks us to see these 'non-specified' mental images as explaining the emblematic quality of Jacobean and Caroline writing (and of the so-called 'stylised' character of pre-Renaissance painting). It is wrong, he says, to think of the verse of metaphysical poets like Crashaw as being lacking in sensuous vividness, just because you would find it hard to 'realise' their more fantastic metaphors. This would be to misunderstand the sixteenth- and seventeenth-century imagination, which worked differently from the modern one. It had not learned to be ruled by the laws of perception, and its creations might be perfectly concrete and vivid (the poet might 'see' them with full realisation) though they had no possible counterpart in the world outside. Indeed, the man of the sixteenth or seventeenth century not only imagined differently, he saw the real world differently too.

> . . . a subject of the first Queen Elizabeth is not at all likely to see the same tree as a subject of the second Queen Elizabeth. The former is likely to see a 'Royal Oak' where the latter will probably see an 'ordinary-looking deciduous tree, perhaps an oak'.[7]

And by this point it has become plain that Nuttall's argument is hopelessly circular. For, as I have said, any idea of *comparing* the mental images of different people must be vain—for a very good reason, that they don't exist. All that exists, in the case of mental images, is a make-believe; and all that can be compared between two cases of private make-believe is what the persons concerned report to you—the words they use. And the words, in the case of literature, are what we started from. We shall not help ourselves to enjoy their words more, or to like Crashaw's 'indecent' conceits better, by asking ourselves what happened to these writers in some 'inner theatre' of imagery.

There is a very funny article by William Empson on the dire consequences of too much attention to 'images' in literature. He relates an alarming anecdote:

> I was much struck recently by a young lady I was tutoring who gave the right answer when confronted with a question from an old 'Practical Criticism' paper; that is, a verse was quoted, and she was to spot the date of it, giving her reasons. Sure enough, she found the images showed that this bit was late eighteenth century; but what the examiners would not have found out was that she had no idea what the verse was saying. It urged you to carry out one of those terrific pieces of landscape gardening, cutting away the side of the hill, digging a lake, planting a forest, to improve the prospect from your country house. She thought the verse was only pictures of scenery, because she never bothered with verbs; to answer questions in the examination you only needed the images.[8]

Unfortunately Empson is not much help to me in my general line of argument, as he seems to feel no difficulty in understanding what 'images' in verse are. He assumes they are the same as 'mental images'. And what he has to say about images, and especially visual images, is that they are useless—'so little use that it is hard to see why they were evolved'. The idea that we *think* in images is, he considers, 'a typical example of primitive thought', like explaining how we hear by saying 'There's a little man in your ear; he listens and he tells you'. And when it comes to poetry, he thinks, 'visual images' contribute very little of value—though 'kinesthetic' ones somewhat more. Empson approaches the whole subject as a defender of argument (or 'argufying') in verse, and hence as an enemy of Symbolism, which frowns on it. The Symbolist doctrine that poems should be made exclusively out of 'images'* seems to him a thoroughly

* Not really an accurate statement of Symbolist doctrine.

cramping and hamstringing prejudice. 'Argufying' has quite as important a place in poetry, and the poems he most likes are full of it. It is Symbolist doctrine, he thinks, that encouraged his pupil not to 'bother with verbs'. This is not quite my own line of argument; but he makes a point, from his own angle, which is part of my own case against the term 'image' in general.

> The doctrine has had bad effects on the readers . . . ; for one thing, if they are given a comparison—for example, 'the mind of man is like the sea'—they tend to forget about the mind, especially the particular mind of the person in view (though the author was using the comparison to tell them something about that); they switch on their stock image, their mental picture-postcard of the eternal sea.[9]

It is usually said in discussions of 'images' and 'imagery' in literature that it is a mistake to think of them as something purely visual. There is also tactual, and aural, and kinetic (or 'kinesthetic') imagery, and imagery of taste and smell. When critics say this, it should, in theory, mean that they have cleared their minds of any association between 'imagery' in literature and 'mental imagery'. For it is clear that there can be no equivalent to 'mental imagery' on the part of the other senses. Putting it simply, we use the eyes in two quite different ways. We receive the same sort of messages through them as we receive through the ears and nose and touch—that is to say, 'sensuous' experiences: in the case of eyes, experiences of light and darkness and colour, and things like 'dazzling' and 'glowing'. But we go on to treat these 'sensuous' visual experiences (as we don't with the experiences of the other senses) as standing for what we *know* about the world. The evidence for what we know about the world—for instance, that there are such things as birds, and that they move through the air on wings, and chirrup and have warm blood and a skeleton inside them—comes in through all the senses, but we have formed the habit of regarding the *appearance* of things as being their reality. We may never have seen a cicada, and have heard it very often, yet we don't regard it as *being* the sound we hear; we think of it as being what we should see if we ever saw one. When Wordsworth asks of the cuckoo

> O Cuckoo! shall I call thee Bird,
> Or but a wandering voice?

we consider this a perfectly sensible question. A cuckoo considered only as what we experience of him through our ears would strike us, as it struck Wordsworth, as a very unreal and ethereal affair:

> No bird, but an invisible thing,
> A voice, a mystery.

And having decided to regard the reality of things as being what we see of them (or would see if they were before our eyes) and to regard the sounds they make, or the way they might feel to our touch or sense of smell, as being merely incidental attributes, we have found it useful, when thinking about things, to pretend to ourselves that we are seeing them in 'our mind's eye'. We find this make-believe, which we call 'mental imagery', a great convenience in reasoning. It is a most obedient servant. We find no difficulty in imagining St. Paul's, then a procession entering St. Paul's, then a man in the procession stumbling on the steps, then all this with an aeroplane passing overhead—no more difficulty than in *thinking* the same things, which it so closely resembles.

No such habit of make-believe exists, for reasons I hope I have made clear, in regard to sounds and smells and touch. We don't reason in sounds and smells; we don't requisition endless new combinations of memories of sound and smells and touch-experiences to illustrate our thought. So there is not, nor can there be, for ordinary persons, aural or olfactory or tactual 'imagery' in the sense normally implied by 'mental imagery'. Even to coin a name for it is rather baffling; yet to call it 'imagery', with the visual implications of that word, is obviously a bit of a paradox. I don't mean to suggest that people can't pretend to themselves that they are hearing sounds 'in their head'; and composers, obviously, can go further and combine imaginary sounds at will. But then in doing so they are not thinking about the world. All that the imaginary sounds represent is real sounds: the sound of a cello or the sound of a clarinet. (And, of course, a 'sound-picture' is only a piece of music arousing visual impressions.)

This is not to say that it is in the nature of things that human beings should attribute reality to visual appearances and those only. People who are blind from birth evidently can't have 'mental imagery' in the usual sense, yet it seems very likely that they too find the habit of make-believe a useful aid to reasoning, and that must mean that they build up a similar system out of experiences of touch. Though, in fact, what such people say is often rather surprising to the sighted. Mlle de Salignac, who had been blind almost from birth, told Diderot that she thought geometry was the ideal science for the blind—for the geometer spends most of his life with his eyes shut anyway. Diderot tested her powers. 'Imagine a cube', he said to her. 'I can see it', she replied. 'Now imagine a point at the centre of the cube.' 'I've done so', she said. 'From the point, draw straight lines to the corners of the cube; that will mean you have divided the cube into sections.' 'Yes, into six equal pyramids,' she replied, 'with identical sides, with the same base as the cube and half its height.' 'Quite right,' said Diderot. 'But where do you see all this?' 'In my head, just like you.' Diderot was startled by her answers, and beat his brains about the mechanics of the thing. How did she do it all without *colour*?

> We form combinations of coloured points; he [the blind person] only forms combinations of touch points, or, to be more exact, of recollected sensations of touch. What goes on in his head cannot be at all the same as goes on in ours; he doesn't imagine; for in order to imagine, you have to establish a coloured background and then separate out certain points from it by supposing them to be of a different colour. Give these points the same colour as the background, and immediately they merge into it, and the figure disappears.[10]

However, perhaps the real lesson of Mlle de Salignac's cool answers is that we should take this whole business of 'mental imagery' lightly. It is plain, and we feel it to be so, that a geometer blind from birth is in just as good a position as anyone else to think about cubes and pyramids. And that being so, the question what sort of 'making-believe' he does to himself in the process begins to look rather frivolous.

V

Thus the associations both with painting and sculpture, and with mental imagery, which the word 'image' carries with it, when used as a substitute for 'metaphor', are irrelevant and misleading. If you are going to use the word in this way, you will have to disentangle it from them. And it's worth remembering that painting, unlike poetry, really is bound up with mental imagery. A painter persuades the spectator, by presenting him with an arrangement of pigments on a canvas, to form mental images of a real scene. The colour and the composition control his mental imagining; they lead his mind towards an overall meaning or significant experience, just as rhythm and syntax and juxtapositions of vocabulary lead the mind of a poetry-reader. The painter has absolute control over the spectator's mental imagery—indeed that is what painting (or at least figurative painting) is about. It is the art of inducing controlled day-dreaming or mental image-making. On the other hand, the mental image-making induced by literature is clearly not an essential part of literature, since it is uncontrolled. As I have said, the most obvious difference between literature and painting is that a writer has only to use a word like 'beechtree' or 'pagoda' for the reader to run up a complete imaginary model of a beech-tree or a pagoda unaided. Thus in so far as a writer is thought of as using 'images', he has no need of a medium—he need not toil over paint and canvas. The word 'image', unlike the word 'metaphor', suggests no connection with the *medium* of poetry, which is words, syntax, and rhythm; and that should make us suspicious of it.

And when you have stripped the words 'image' and 'imagery', as used in literary criticism, of their associations with painting and sculpture, and also of their associations with mental imagery, you really haven't much left. Indeed, if you are trying to use the words as a substitute for 'metaphor', I don't think you have anything left. Any extra implications the words lend to the idea conveyed by 'metaphor' are false and misleading.

There appear to be only two ways in which the words can convey a definite and useful meaning in literary criticism. First the familiar eighteenth-century sense, in which an 'image' means something directly painterly—as when, in a descriptive poem, the writer pretends that he is imitating a painter, and 'paints' such a scene as the artist might have chosen to paint. And here the words 'paint' and 'painter' are meant no more literally than when Fielding described himself, when writing *Tom Jones*, as a 'historian'. It is a pleasant fancy about the writer's professional role, and does not imply that what he actually produces has any resemblance to a painting constructed of oils and canvas, a painting full of visual relationships which it may take hours or a lifetime to explore.

Secondly, there is the important new sense in which the Imagist poets used the word 'image'—i.e. as a term to denote a whole Imagist poem. And here the implication is that a poem of this sort has a kind of resemblance to a painting in that—unlike traditional poems—it works (or pretends to work) *instantaneously*, without temporal progression. By expunging as far as possible all the sequential parts of discourse—narrative, conventional syntax, etc.—it imitates that characteristic feature of a painting that it is present to the spectator all at once. From this point of view, but only from this point of view, there is a loose resemblance between such a poem and a painting, and it is therefore apt enough to call it an 'image'.*

However, neither of these two senses of the words 'image' or 'imagery' has any intrinsic connection with metaphor or comparison. And I think that nothing but confusion come from using them in any sense that does. But at this point we had better take a look at the history of the words.

---

* See pp. 38–48 for a longer discussion of Imagist poetry.

2

HOW THE WORDS DEVELOPED

1 EARLY HISTORY

Historically, the word 'imagery', at least until the eighteenth century, had a fairly uncomplicated sense. It was applied not to literature, but to things which were by definition pictorial —like tapestry, paintings or sculptures. It was, from medieval times, the word you used for the design of a tapestry:

> She wafe a cloth of silke all white
> With letters and ymagery.
>
> (Gower, quoted by *O.E.D.*)

and the definition still current in most seventeenth- and eighteenth-century dictionaries was 'painted or carved work of images'. Puttenham was using the word in the same simple sense when he said 'when we liken an human person to another in countenance, stature, speach or other qualities, it is called . . . resemblaunce by imagerie or pourtrait'.[1]

The word 'image' has always been richer in meaning, and from early times the sense of 'an artificial imitation or representation' (as in 'graven image'), or 'optical appearance' (as in 'I saw my own image in a glass'), or 'mental picture' (as in 'Why do I yield to that suggestion/Whose horrid image doth unfix my hair?'), has merged into the sense of 'emblem', 'epitome' or 'typical embodiment' (as in 'God created man in his own image', or 'Mr. Sampson . . . sat transfixed, an image of half amused astonishment'). And between these two groups of senses there is room for a wide variety of overlapping meanings. Like 'imagery', the word 'image' was not normally applied to literature, though it (or rather its Latin equivalent '*imago*') makes a brief appearance in Wilson's *Arte of Rhetorique*

(1562), as meaning a kind of portraiture by comparison (his definition gets rather dark towards the end).

> *Ressemblyng of thinges,* is a comparyinge or likenyng of looke, with looke, shape, with shape, and one thynge with another. As when I see one in a great heate, and fiercely set upon his enemie, I might saie, he lets flee at hym like a Dragon. Or thus, He lokes like a Tiger, a man would think he would eate one, his countenance is so ougle . . . By this figure called in Latine *Imago,* that is to saie an Ymage, we mighte compare one manne with another, as Salust compareth Caesar and Cato together, or we mighte heape many men together, and prove by large rehersall, any thyng that we would, the whiche of the Logicians is called induccion.[2]

However, in eighteenth-century dictionaries the word 'image' was generally defined in two clear ways: first, as the kind of thing produced by a sculptor or a painter ('a representation or likeness of a thing, either natural or artificial; a statue or a picture'[3]); and secondly (this was the only literary sense given), as a feature of rhetoric—a description or evocation of a scene or action so vivid that it makes the listener almost believe he is actually witnessing it.

> such discourse as some persons, when by a kind of enthusiasm or extraordinary commotion of the soul, they seem to see things whereof they speak.[4]

And behind this rhetorical sense there seems to be lurking some long-standing tradition about the classical orators—who, no doubt, had a trick of pretending, at a certain point in their speech, that they were rapt and possessed by an absent scene.

Abraham Rees, in his *Cyclopaedia . . . of Arts, Sciences and Literature* (1819), quotes Cicero's 'elegant' description of the barbarity of Verres ('*Ipse flammatus scelere et furore, in forum venit; toto ex ore crudelitas emanabat,* etc.') as an example of 'hypotyposis' or 'imagery' and says that 'this figure is peculiarly suited for drawing characters'. Of 'images' in rhetoric he says, paraphrasing a passage in Longinus, that they 'have a very different use from what they have among the poets: the end principally proposed in poetry is astonishment and surprise; whereas the thing chiefly aimed at in prose is to paint things naturally, and to show them clearly. They have this, however, in common that they both tend to move, each in their kind.'

Ray Frazer, who has traced the origin of the word 'image' as a literary term in a very interesting article,[5] says that this use of it came in at the time of Dryden and the Royal Society, as part of a reaction against rhetoric. 'Rhetoric to them was a kind of black art, a hangover from the scholastic Dark Ages, a systematic program of deception which covered honest "things" with doubtful "words".' There was, he says, 'a curiously urgent demand for "perspicuity" after 1660' and it expressed itself chiefly 'in a hostility towards rhetoric, towards figures and particularly towards metaphor. The proscription of rhetoric proscribed the chief critical vocabulary of the past. *Image* was one of the terms to fill the vacuum.' It came in, that is to say, as part of an early and minor 'positivist' revolution.

Frazer goes on to show that the word 'image', as first used as a term of literary criticism, was particularly connected with a new kind of descriptive poem, based on the Lockian theory of associationism. 'In a few years after Denham descriptive and reflective poems were structured not by logic but by association.' Poets like Young felt that they were getting away from the fabrication of elegantly artificial products and responding instead to what came to them from outside. 'As the occasion of this poem was real, not fictitious,' wrote Young of his *Night Thoughts*, 'so the method pursued in it was rather imposed by what spontaneously arose in the author's mind on that occasion, than meditated or designed.' And the reader of descriptive poems such as these was expected to repeat the poet's response to the outside world in reverse order.

> According to the theory of the association of ideas, the appreciation of art was the exact reversal of its creation: the reader's spaniel followed the writer's back through the fields of memory.[6]

Frazer speaks elsewhere in his article as though the word 'image' was already, at this early period, widely used as a direct synonym for the old rhetorical terms 'simile' and 'metaphor'. And it certainly was sometimes used in this way, as was the word 'imagery', for instance when Dennis says:

> No sort of imagery can ever be the language of grief. If a man complains in simile, I either laugh or sleep.[7]

However, so far as I have been able to find, this sense was not recognised in eighteenth-century dictionaries. And the sense uppermost in writers' minds during the eighteenth century, when using the words as literary terms, seems to have been directly pictorial, with no implication of comparison: a scenic or statuesque sense, as when Dr. Johnson speaks of 'scenes of imagery'. A writer, when he produced a vivid 'image' of something, was thought to be behaving much like the classical orator as described by Longinus. He was evoking something so vividly that the reader forgot he was reading a book and imagined he was actually present before a real scene or object.

> The power of language to raise emotions, depends entirely on the raising of such lively and distinct images as are described: the reader's passions are never sensibly moved, till he be thrown into a kind of reverie; in which state, forgetting himself, and forgetting that he is reading, he conceives every incident as passing in his presence, precisely as if he were an eye-witness.[8]

Or alternatively he was producing the literary equivalent of an allegorical statue or monument—a simple extension of the old dictionary definition 'painted or carved work of images'. Both senses are present when Nicholas Rowe writes of Viola's speech in *Twelfth Night* (though of course the reference to a monument is already there in Shakespeare).

> His [Shakespeare's] Images are indeed ev'ry where so lively, that the Thing he would represent stands before you, and you possess ev'ry Part of it. I will venture to point out one more, which is, I think, as strong and as uncommon as anything I ever saw; 'tis an Image of Patience. Speaking of a Maid in Love, he says,
>
> . . . She never told her Love,
> But let Concealment, like a Worm i' th' Bud
> Feed on her Damask Cheek. She pin'd in Thought,
> And sate like *Patience* on a Monument,
> Smiling at *Grief*.
>
> What an Image is here given! and what a Task would it have been for the greatest Masters of *Greece* and *Rome* to

have express'd the Passions design'd by this Sketch of Statuary?[9]

Of course, the word 'image' and 'imagery' were often used in the eighteenth century in discussing passages which contained similes and metaphors, but they did not therefore necessarily refer to the similes and metaphors as such. A reviewer writing in *The Critical Review* of 1793 about Wordsworth's *An Evening Walk* says:

> . . . we are compensated by that merit which a poetical tale most values, new and picturesque imagery.

and he quotes the picture of the setting sun:

> A long blue bar its aegis orb divides,
> And breaks the spreading of its golden tides.

and the one of the heron, which

> Springs upwards, darting his long neck before.

The first contains metaphors, and the second one does not—or at least only a dead one; and this difference clearly is of no importance to the reviewer. It is interesting that a remark of Dryden's, 'I wish there may be in this poem any instance of good imagery', which is quoted in the *O.E.D.* as an instance of the word 'imagery' used in the sense of 'metaphors', is cited by Dr. Johnson, in his dictionary, as illustrating the use of the word to mean 'descriptions'—'such descriptions as force the image of the thing described upon the mind'. And as late as the 1830s we find Wordsworth still arguing in favour of a purely pictorial sense for the word 'imagery':

> S——, in the work you mentioned to me, confounds *imagery* and *imagination*. Sensible objects really existing, and felt to exist, are *imagery*; and they may form the materials of a descriptive poem, where objects are delineated as they are. Imagination is a subjective term: it deals with objects not as they are, but as they appear to the mind of the poet.[10]

It is really through the influence of Coleridge that a permanent association between the words 'image' and 'imagery' and metaphors and similes came to be set up, and it occurred as a byproduct of development in another word: Imagination. For Coleridge himself, the simple pictorial definition of the word is still strong. He writes, for instance, in Chapter 15 of *Biographia Literaria*: 'Images, however beautiful, though faithfully copied from nature, and as accurately represented in words, do not of themselves characterise the poet.' That 'copied from nature' is perfectly literal and Wordsworthian and contains no allusion to metaphor. And throughout his famous analysis of 'The specific symptoms of poetic power elucidated in a critical analysis of Shakespeare's *Venus and Adonis*, and *Rape of Lucrece*' he is using 'image' and 'imagery' in their normal Augustan sense. He is thinking of how a dramatic poet like Shakespeare, where he cannot depend on the assistance of actors, may fall back as a substitute on his so-called 'painterly' powers. Shakespeare, he feels, is determined to *show*, to be scenic, to act the omnipresent observer and theatrical producer. He attempts by means of a 'series and never broken chain of imagery, always vivid and, because unbroken, minute; by the highest effort of the picturesque in words, of which words are capable' to provide a substitute for the 'visual language' which in his plays he was entitled to expect from his actors.

However, his main subject in this essay is the Imagination, which, he says, works by a process of combining and fusing, by the 'balance or reconcilement of opposite or discordant qualities'. And one of the ways in which the Imagination reveals itself is by its power of modifying 'images' (such as otherwise would have been perfectly in place in a book of topography) by a predominant passion, 'or by associated thoughts or images awakened by that passion'. And since one of the main means by which the Imagination displays its 'modifying' and 'fusing' power, according to Coleridge, is through similes and metaphors, the words 'image' and 'imagery', through being named in such close conjunction with them in these famous pages, came to be bound up more closely with them.

By the middle of the nineteenth century the words 'image' and 'imagery' were regularly used as a comprehensive synonym for 'similes' and 'metaphors' and this definition had reached the dictionaries. Joseph Worcester's *Dictionary of the English Language* (Boston, 1863) defines 'Imagery' thus:

> 4 (Rhet.) Lively descriptions in writing or in speech; figurative language.

> It is a generic term for similes, allegories, metaphors, and such other rhetorical figures as denote similitude and comparison. *Brande*.

And W. T. Brande and G. W. Cox, in their *Dictionary of Science, Literature, and Art* (1866) say under the word 'Image':

> In Rhetoric, a term somewhat loosely used; it appears generally to denote a metaphor dilated, and rendered a more complete picture by the assemblage of various ideas through which the same metaphor continues to run, yet not sufficiently expanded to form an allegory.

However, the words 'image' and 'imagery' had not so far supplanted the older and more technical terms; and to the extent that they were used as a synonym for them, they kept a fairly matter-of-fact and technical flavour, as terms denoting 'figures of speech'. Though the career of the word 'Imagination' had disturbed them in its triumphant ascent, it had not raised them to its own heightened plane.

Meanwhile, in keeping with the anti-Augustan emphasis on minute and scientific observation which you find in Ruskin, Tennyson and the Pre-Raphaelites, critics were insisting more and more on 'distinct images' (in a painterly sense) as the stuff of good writing, or on the power to conceive 'distinct images' as the precondition of it. G. H. Lewes, in an essay 'Distinct Images Necessary' later published in *The Principles of Success in Literature* (1898), says:

> an artist produces an effect in virtue of the distinctness with which he sees the objects he represents, seeing them not vaguely as in vanishing apparitions, but steadily, and in their most characteristic relations. To this Vision he adds artistic skill with which to make us see.

He attacks the showy 'imagery' of bad contemporary writers as a betrayal of the prime duty of writers—to *see*.

> What the majority of modern verse writers call 'imagery' is not the product of imagination, but a restless pursuit of comparison and a lax use of language. Instead of presenting us with an image of the object, they present us with something which they tell us is like the object—which it rarely is. The thing itself has no clear significance to them, it is only

a text for the display of their ingenuity. If, however, we turn from poetasters to poets, we see great accuracy in depicting the things themselves or their suggestions, so that we may be certain the things presented themselves in the field of the poet's vision, and were painted because seen.

In fact, though, the word 'image' drifts pretty loosely from sense to sense in Lewes, sometimes standing for 'vision' (Scott's 'image' of Mucklebackit and Saladin), sometimes for 'epitome' (a description by Wordsworth represents his 'image of November'), and sometimes for 'symbol':

> At the outset we must come to an understanding as to this word 'image', and endeavour to free the word 'vision' from all equivoque. If these words were understood literally there would be an obvious absurdity in speaking of an image of a sound, or of seeing an emotion. Yet if by means of symbols the effect of a sound is produced in us, or the psychological state of any human being is rendered intelligible to us, we are said to have images of these things, which the poet has imagined. It is because the eye is the most valued and intellectual of our senses that the majority of metaphors are borrowed from its sensations. Language, after all, is only the use of symbols, and Art also can only affect us through symbols. If a phrase can summon a terror resembling that summoned by the danger which it indicates, a man is said to *see* the danger.

He reproves Burke for failing, in his attack on the prestige of 'sensible images' in literature (see pp. 10–11), to see that tones, looks, and gestures are also 'images': they are the 'intelligible symbols of passion—"images" in the true sense—just as words are the intelligible symbols of ideas. The subject-matter is as clearly expressed by the one as the other.'

Later in the century, the word 'image' was given a new and rich reverberation by the Symbolist movement, especially in the person of Yeats. But here we are moving rather outside the word's development as a literary term. Yeats, who is very consistent in his way of using the word, always gives it a Blakian and magical sense, with no direct reference to the literary medium. For Yeats, 'images' are the furniture of the great memory of Nature. They are the patterns of the Great

Mind, from which all things are created and recreated, or they are the signs and symbols with which men make contact with these patterns.

> Mystics of many countries and many centuries have spoken of this memory; and the honest men and charlatans, who keep the magical traditions which will some day be studied as a part of folk-lore, base most that is of importance in their claims upon this memory. I have read of it in *Paracelsus* and in some Indian book that describes the people of past days as still living within it, 'thinking the thought and doing the deed'. And I have found it in the 'Prophetic Books' of William Blake, who calls its images 'the bright sculptures of Los's Hall'; and says that all events, 'all love stories', renew themselves from those images.[11]

Conceived in this magical Yeatsian way, the word 'image' is to be understood in an idolatrous sense. Like idols of wood and stone, 'images' are seen as drawing down gods and supernatural influences among men. So, indeed, in their own way, do all the elements of works of art, according to Yeats.

> All sounds, all colours, all forms, either because of their preordained energies or because of long association, evoke indefinable and yet precise emotions, or, as I prefer to think, call down among us certain disembodied powers, whose footsteps over our hearts we call emotions . . . The same relation exists between all portions of every work of art, whether it be an epic or song, and the more perfect it is, and the more various and numerous the elements that have flowed into its perfection, the more powerful will be the emotion, the power, the god it calls among us.[12]

Where Yeats wants to talk, not of the sources of art and the laws of being, but of literature as a medium, his preferred word is 'symbol'. The literary significance of the word 'image' for him is not as a piece of terminology but as an expression of discontentment with literature. 'I seek an image, not a book.'

It is this Yeatsian sense of the word 'image'—which, as I say, has nothing directly to do with literature as a medium—that Frank Kermode has in mind in his book *Romantic Image* (1957). And it is an objection to this brilliant book that at first reading you might not realise how much Kermode's way of using the word 'image', as conveying the whole complex of Symbolist ideas about a work of art, is his own and not that of the writers he is discussing. Arthur Symons, for instance, does not often use the word 'image'. For him the key word is 'symbol', as for Pater it is 'vision'.

Moreover it is the word 'image', in this complex modern sense, which does half the work for Kermode in showing that the Romantics and the Symbolists belong to the same tradition. And there are things which worry one about this view. It was an illuminating idea of Kermode's to explain the 'wan face' of Keats's Moneta as a representation of the 'Image', and so as all one with the mask-like 'death-in-life' faces of Rossetti's Lilith and Pater's Monna Lisa. But there is something not quite right with his interpretation of Keats. It leaves out his all-important *philanthropic* side, which is what links him with Wordsworth and Coleridge and separates him from Pater:

> 'None can usurp this height,' returned that shade,
> 'But those to whom the miseries of the world
> Are misery, and will not let them rest.'

The word 'image' is a great concealer of differences, especially when it has a capital letter. And one remembers that it was Coleridge who made a remark about 'the dangers of thinking in images'.

2 RÉMY DE GOURMONT

Nobody is likely to care very much what G. H. Lewes thought about the principles of literature, except as a matter of history. However, the demand for 'distinct images' in literature which we saw him making, became, in one version or another, a major theme of modernist literary theory. It was taken up, in a recognisably modern manner, by Rémy de Gourmont; and though I have not been concerned with the fate of the words 'image' and 'imagery' in other cultures, Gourmont had so much influence on Eliot and Pound that it makes sense to discuss him here. Moreover, he deserves more than historical treatment; he needs to be argued with.

Gourmont wrote as a survivor of the Symbolist movement, but, as Donald Davie has pointed out,[13] he had strong eighteenth-century sympathies—though with the eighteenth century of Buffon rather than of *Télémaque* and *Rasselas*. And he finds it quite natural to speak, like any Augustan critic, of the writer as 'painting' things. Gourmont, in *Le Problème du style*, distinguishes two kinds of author—the 'visual' or 'sensorial' writer on the one hand, and on the other the '*idéo-émotif*' writer (the writer who deals in ideas and feelings). Chateaubriand is the ideal 'visual' writer; his mind is stored with innumerable exact visual observations, and by a recombination of such 'images' he is able to create artistic forms which embody his whole sensibility (leaving him nothing left for life). Musset, on the other hand, is an '*idéo-émotif*' writer; he remembers, not what he has seen, but only what he has felt, and his words do not embody his experience but merely allude to it—so that when the fugitive association linking the words to the experience is broken, all that is left is an empty bottle, a savourless husk. The 'visual' or 'sensorial' writer (the only true kind, according to Gourmont) has the capacity to 'lie' (lying being the basis of all art and civilisation), and he is adept at inventing new metaphors. The '*idéo-émotif*' writer is 'sincere'—that is to say, he is imitative and uncreative—and, lacking the visual memory which alone can provide material for new metaphoric invention, has to content himself with stock phrases.

Metaphor, in its fully developed form, says Gourmont, is a modern discovery. It was unknown to Homer. For Homer, impressions occur successively, and he describes them in orderly succession; so that it would be quite easy to illustrate the *Iliad* by a series of panels or diptychs. He was incapable of the 'lying' represented by metaphor; the most he could rise to was the simile.

> Comparison is the elementary form of the visual imagination. It precedes metaphor—which is a comparison in which one of the terms is missing unless indeed the two terms are fused into one.[14]

It is only in the present age, with its capacity for synaesthesia (i.e. for interpreting the experiences of one sense in terms of those of another) that the full resources of metaphor have been understood. And from this discovery (which was as major a discovery as the invention of the vault by the Romans) there was no turning back; the similes of Homer must henceforth always seem naive to us.

> We have no need, any longer, to establish first of all the literal fact which we want to record, then to mention something analogous which explains, or reinforces, or qualifies it; the art has been acquired, once and for all, of announcing two facts at one blow, intermingling them with as much skill as our particular talent allows us.[15]

We have been given mastery of a marvellous form of 'lying', unknown to the ancients: 'every metaphor is a tale; complicated stories, metamorphoses, rapes, love-affairs, conquests are given us in a few words, or even in a single one'. And this kind of lying, the perquisite of the masters of metaphor, is beyond the powers of painting to illustrate.

> Flaubert, who has infinite talent for lying, and therefore for art itself, is not being literal when he writes: 'The elephants . . . the spurs on their chests like the prows of ships cut through the cohorts; they rolled back in great waves.' He is able to amalgamate the two images (elephants and cohorts, ships and waves) so well only because he has seen them simultaneously. What he gives us is not two designs fitting symmetrically one over the other, but the confusion—visually absurd and artistically admirable—of a double and cloudy sensation . . . Try to represent the image of elephant-prows, of cohort-waves, visually! You would need a stormy sea which was a real sea and yet one not made of waves, but of soldiers' chests and heads; and elephants who, whilst still remaining elephants, would also be ships. . . . Images can only be translated into painting—a literal, and indeed geometric, art—when they are not metaphors.[16]

Gourmont, as we see, tends to use 'image' in a double sense. The 'sensorial' or 'visual' writer looks at the picture-show of 'images' in his head (the fruit of patient observation) and translates it into literature (according to his degree of skill) by newly invented metaphors, also to be called 'images'. Though he may also produce 'images' which are not metaphors but simple transcriptions of observed reality:

> The Chateaubriand of the *Mémoires d'outre-tombe* is a flood of metaphoric iridescence. With him perfumes, sounds, colours, savours and experiences of touch mingle in perpetual synaethesias . . . But from time to time the image is a simple

> transcription, detail by detail, of observed facts. How many times have I not seen, like him, from the house next to his in the Rue du Bac, the *same* swallows 'plunge twittering into the holes in the walls'.[17]

And if his theory of literature, as a whole, strikes us as inadequate despite the brilliant insights taken up by Eliot, it is somewhere in its talk of 'images' that it goes wrong.

For to begin with, though he constantly talks of the writer as 'painting' reality, the analogy with painting breaks down just at the crucial point—where he is describing the modern discovery of 'pure', liberated, metaphor. Homer can be illustrated, but Flaubert, as he admits, cannot.

Again, he remarks that a purely 'visual' or 'concrete' style—a style fashioned exclusively from the pure ore of new 'images'—would be incomprehensible. You need an admixture of the 'banal' and the 'vulgar' to cement the hewn blocks of stone. And this view, by which everything in literature except 'images' is so much base material, is such a denial of the indivisibility of works of art as to sound like rejecting literature for something else. There must be something wrong with any view of literature which elevates one feature of it—whether its 'images' or its moral teaching or its 'music'—into its sole *raison d'être*, and degrades all its other features into humble tools or tedious necessities. It leads to talking about all these other features as a mere matter of 'skill'. Whereas it is just this 'skill', or the fruits of it, that we are interested in as critics, since it constitutes what is on the page. To talk about a writer's 'skill' is to talk either about what is almost everything for the critic, or about some quality of his as a person—whether he has a 'gift for literature' or not—which is not the business of the critic at all but of the biographer.

Another obvious weakness in Gourmont's theory, by which metaphors are made the heart and *raison d'être* of literature, comes out in what he says about live and dead metaphors. Critics, says Gourmont, have written of French writers of the pre-Romantic period—of Bossuet, La Bruyère and Fénelon, etc.—as *abstract* writers; but this is an illusion. These writers invented a great many vivid 'images': it is merely that their 'images' have turned into clichés through the passage of time and over-use by later writers. (Trace the history of those faded flowers of speech beloved of cliché-mongering politicians and you will find their fresh and glowing originals in Saint-Simon or La Bruyère.) Gourmont pictures an endless cycle in which sensations give rise to 'image-words', 'image-words' turn into 'idea-words', and 'idea-words' turn into 'sentiment-words', whereafter they either vanish into the abyss of nothingness or pass into action—from which new sensations will be born, and the whole cycle (a cycle by which all art, all civilisation, is produced) can begin anew.

But whatever is true of language, the point about major literature and art is that it doesn't lose its freshness or turn into cliché through imitation or the passage of time. Great art, by its form, has a way of fixing and sealing its effects, so that any novelty it contains goes on being novel and does not fade into the commonplace.* So if metaphors are prisoners of a cycle of birth and decay, and have no virtue to retain their novelty, then metaphors, in themselves, are plainly not literature, or the essence' or 'heart' of literature; and metaphor-making (or in Gourmont's words 'image-making') cannot be the essential activity of the writer.

Finally, of course, there is a simple historical objection to Gourmont's theory that the power to exploit and understand 'pure' metaphor is a modern acquisition, and an aspect of the modern (i.e. nineteenth-century) capacity for synaesthesia. He is taking his evidence from French literature, forgetting Shakespeare, whose mature work is full of metaphors more advanced than any in Chateaubriand or Flaubert.

3 THE IMAGISTS

A further, and major, development in the meaning of the word 'image' came about with the Imagist movement. And if (as it seems to me) the word as used by English nineteenth-century critics, and by Gourmont likewise, always creates muddle and would have been better translated into more precise words like

---

* See an excellent passage in W. K. Wimsatt's *The Verbal Icon* (1954), pp. 127–8, on the 'dead metaphor' (which he defines as 'a collapsed metaphor, one in which A and B have come together so completely that only one is left holding the field') and on the poem as 'a structure of verbal meaning' which keeps a metaphor alive and prevents this happening.

'metaphor', 'symbol', 'epitome', etc., with the Imagist movement it undoubtedly took on a new and fruitful sense.

It is best to understand the Imagist theorists, when talking of 'the Image', as referring to a complete Imagist poem (they have, significantly, not much use for the word 'imagery'). An image, according to Pound, is that which 'presents an intellectual and an emotional complex in an instant of time . . . It is the presentation of such a "complex" instantaneously which gives that sense of sudden liberation; that sense of freedom from time limits and space limits; that sense of sudden growth, which we experience in the presence of the greatest works of art.' And, as he remarks in a note to the essay 'Vorticism', there is no reason why you should not have a *long* Imagist poem; the poem can still be single 'image'.

> I am often asked whether there can be a long imagist or vorticist poem. The Japanese, who evolved the hokku, evolved also the Noh plays. In the best 'Noh', the whole play may consist of one image. I mean it is gathered about one image. Its unity consists in one image, enforced by movement and music.[18]

Used in that way, the word has a certain aptness. For a poem conceived as that which 'presents an intellectual and emotional complex in an instant of time' has something important in common with a painting or a sculpture—the quality of *instantaneity.* An Imagist poem, unlike traditional poems, works, or pretends to work, instantaneously, without temporal progression, just as a painting or a sculpture works. A painting is 'given' to the spectator as an instantaneous whole. He will have to scan it, of course; but he can begin scanning where he chooses. He does not have to follow a fixed temporal sequence, like that imposed by words in a sentence or notes in music. And the Imagist poet, finding this 'instantaneity' of painting attractive, attempts to bring poetry nearer to painting by playing down as far as possible the sequential aspect of language. He expunges all 'unnecessary' words; he cuts away, as far as possible, all conventional syntax and all the narrative and sequential parts of discourse—in order to give the 'sense of freedom from time limits and space limits'.

The analogy with painting is helpful, partly because it is fairly remote. It is only as a fiction or figure of speech that an

Imagist poem—even from this point of view—can be said to be like a painting. What complicates the issue, however, is that Pound, in creating his own poetics, was under a strong desire to find common ground with post-impressionist painters and sculptors, and to move nearer to them in his art. His memoir of the sculptor Gaudier-Brzeska (1916)—his chief Vorticist manifesto, and a work written at a high pitch of creative intensity—shows him constantly groping after an an unseizable identity between the plastic arts and poetry.

His own bent as a poet led him towards taking beauty from the visible world—not as one describing the world, but as one striking out new forms in face of it. And the dilemma or paradox that he is brilliantly wrestling with in *Gaudier-Brzeska* is the one discussed in my opening pages—i.e. that a poet, in order to present the visible universe, seems to have to offer *two* heterogeneous things, in place of the painter or sculptor's one. 'Pourquoi doubler l'image?' he quotes Henri-Martin Barzun as asking. Poetry ought to be able to present objects directly, just like the plastic arts. Yet poetry, especially poetry concerned with the visible world, seems to need to work with metaphors, and metaphors involve two things, two unlike things (for things have to be unlike in kind for it to be worth comparing them).

Pound defines the differences between poetry and the plastic arts in a series of propositions:

> The pine-tree in mist upon the far hill looks like a fragment of Japanese armour.
>
> The beauty of this pine-tree in the mist is not caused by its resemblance to the plates of the armour.
>
> The armour, if it be beautiful at all, is not beautiful *because* of its resemblance to the pine in the mist.
>
> In either case the beauty, in so far as it is beauty of form, is the result of 'planes in relation'.
>
> The tree and the armour are beautiful because their diverse planes overlie in a certain manner.
>
> There is the sculptor's or the painter's *key*. The presentation of this beauty is primarily his job. And the 'poet'? 'Pourquoi doubler l'image?' asks Barzun in declaiming against this 'poésie farcie de "comme" '. The poet, whatever his 'figure of speech', will not arrive by doubling or confusing an image.

> Still the artist, working in words only, may cast on the reader's mind a more vivid image of either the armour or the pine by mentioning them close together or by using some device of simile or metaphor, that is a legitimate procedure of his art, for he works not with planes or with colours but with the names of objects and of properties. It is his business so to use, so to arrange, these names as to cast a more definite image than the layman can cast . . .[19]

Thus, whereas the painter or the sculptor can make the pine-tree alone, or the armour alone, his subject, the poet cannot very well present the one without the aid of the other—he has to convey their separate beauties by 'mentioning them close together', or by drawing a metaphor from one to the other.

Pound evidently finds this need on the part of literature to present *two* things—two heterogeneous things—a worry, and tries to circumvent it in several ways. He says that 'the "one-image" poem is a form of super-position, that is to say one idea on top of another'—which is as much as to say that it becomes one thing instead of two. He is writing these words in connection with the celebrated poem 'In a Station of the Metro':

> The apparition of these faces in the crowd;
> Petals on a wet, black bough.

The original impulse behind the poem, his emotion at seeing a row of beautiful faces on the 'metro' platform at La Concorde, first embodied itself in his mind as a pattern of little splotches of colour, and really, he says, should have culminated in a painting. The two-line poem which he finally arrived at instead, eighteen months later, by paring down some thirty lines, was meant to have not only the intensity and concentration which were the aim of Vorticist art, but to have the character of a *single*, unmixed thing, like the original pattern of colours. The two halves of the metaphor were to disappear in a perfect super-imposition.

Pound's attitude to metaphor, during his Imagist and Vorticist periods, is coloured by his desire to play down the difference between poetry and the plastic arts. He apparently shares Fenollosa's belief that 'Metaphor, the revealer of nature, is the very substance of poetry'—a view he also found support for in T. E. Hulme and Rémy de Gourmont. But to have value, he holds, metaphors must be functional, not ornamental.[20]

> In Guido Cavalcanti the 'figure', the strong metamorphic or picturesque expression, is there with a purpose to convey or to interpret a definite meaning. In Petrarch it is ornamental, the prettiest ornament he could find . . .[21]

And in apparent conflict with his high valuation of metaphor, he considers it as one of the perpetual vices of writers to think that one thing must be represented 'in terms of' another. For this is a violation of nature, an infringement of the integrity and independent selfhood of existing things. This goes with his antipathy towards Symbolism. (Though I think he never fully understood Symbolist theory. For him, coming at the fag-end of the movement, Symbolism, with its 'mushy technique', represented everything that Vorticism existed to destroy.) He is ready, however, to toy with a belief in a sort of 'permanent metaphor'—which is 'symbolism in its profounder sense. It is not necessarily a belief in a permanent world, but it is a belief in that direction.' The point, for him, is that metaphors should express a reality, something that is permanently true of nature, or of man's relation to nature. And as a consequence, he would be happier if he could strip metaphors of their dependent status as 'figures of speech'. He wants them to 'come true', to enjoy a kind of presentative actuality, like something in painting or sculpture.

The formal techniques of Imagist poetry come in to reinforce this. For if you treat a metaphor or comparison as the core of a poem and pare away all 'unnecessary' discursive structure, the metaphor begins to cease to look like a metaphor. It is the context which forces one half of a metaphor into the subordinate role of a 'vehicle', or *façon de parler*, for the other half, the 'tenor'—the thing which you are 'really' talking about. Remove the context and the two halves have equal status. And indeed it is a fact that Imagist poets sometimes produce poems in which you don't know which is the 'real' subject, and which is the thing it is being likened to. I had always read 'H.D.'s 'Oread'

> Whirl up sea,
> whirl your pointed pines,
> splash your great pines
> on our rocks,
> hurl your green over us,
> cover us with your pools of fir.

as being about the sea, as compared with a forest, but C. K. Stead[22] reads it as being about a forest, as compared with the sea. But in fact it is both—and you don't need to decide which.

Again, the word 'metamorphosis', which Pound uses in speaking of Cavalcanti's metaphors, has its special echo for the reader of the *Cantos*. The idea of metamorphosis is central to Pound's own poetic, whether he is writing a *hokku*-like two-line poem or the *Cantos* themselves. His remark about 'In a Station of the Metro'—'In a poem of this sort one is trying to record the precise instant when a thing outward and objective transforms itself, or darts into a thing inward and subjective'—is a key to the Ovidian metamorphoses which figure so largely in the *Cantos*. The fugal 'counter-subject' in the *Cantos*, as he explains in a letter to his father in 1927,[23] is 'The magic moment or moment of metamorphosis, bust thru from quotidien into "divine or permanent world". Gods, etc.' His using of the word 'metamorphosis' in speaking of figures of speech, is another case of his wanting to give them a justification in experience and in the nature of things—somewhat as Rémy de Gourmont tried to justify metaphors on evolutionary grounds, as being an expression of modern man's newly acquired faculty for synaesthesia. There is a strong wish on Pound's part for metaphor to be revelatory, and not merely a literary device or a part of language and discourse.

We should also remember, in reading the passage in which Pound defines the beauty available to the painter and sculptor (as opposed to the poet), as consisting in 'planes in relation', how often he (and other Imagist poets too) attempt to poach on the painter's and sculptor's preserves. Unable to have this kind of beauty of 'planes in relation' in the *form* of their verses, they compensate by having it in their subject-matter. In speaking of the 'common grounds of the "arts" ', Pound insists that 'It does *not* mean that the poet is to describe post-impressionist pictures'; but he does not always obey his own warning. It is because of the attraction for him of the sculptor's 'planes in relation' that he writes, in Canto XVII:

> marble leaf, over leaf,
> silver, steel over steel,
> silver beaks rising and crossing,
> prow set against prow,
> stone, ply over ply,

or

ply over ply, thin glitter of water;
Brook film bearing white petals.
(Canto IV)

This love of overlapping surfaces and lattice patterns, as a *subject*, runs throughout the *Cantos*, and it is also characteristic of 'H.D.'

where rollers shot with blue
cut under deeper blue
('The Shrine')

We were enchanted with the fields,
the tufts of coarse grass
in the shorter grass.
('The Helmsman')

each leaf
cuts another leaf on the grass,
shadow seeks shadow
('Evening')

Again, Pound's championing of the 'Image', and his insistence on the poet's 'casting a more precise image of beauty upon the mind of the spectator, than the spectator can get of himself', is coloured by his own very special metaphysical concern with the nature of light. It is plain that he himself inhabits, by natural endowment as well as intellectual conviction, the world which he says modern man has lost:

> the radiant world where one thought cuts through another with clean edge, a world of moving energies '*mezzo oscuro rade*', '*risplende in se perpetuale effecto*', magnetisms that take form, that are seen, or that border on the visible, the matter of Dante's *paradiso*, the glass under water, the form that seems a form seen in a mirror . . .[24]

And in thinking of the word 'phanopoeia', which he later adopted in place of 'image' (feeling that the latter had become too much identified with the 'stationary' image, leaving out of account the 'moving' one) we are reminded of those extraordinary little poems in *Lustra* to which he also gives the general title *Phanopoeia*, and in which he gives his imagination free rein among optical phantasmata—that sort of firework display of haloing and after-images one sometimes sees through half-shut eyes or after pressing the eyeballs.

The swirl of light follows me through the square,
The smoke of incense
Mounts from the four horns of my bed-posts,
The water-jet of gold light bears us up through
the ceiling;
Lapped in the gold-coloured flame I descend through
the aether.
The silver ball forms in my hand,
It falls and rolls to your feet.

Pound's account of Imagist or Vorticist poetry fails, moreover, to mention one important aspect of it, which belongs purely to literature and has no counterpart in painting or sculpture—I mean, syntax. If Symbolist poetry employs 'pseudo-syntax'—a full and elaborate syntax which is only pretending to do the normal work of syntax *—then Imagist poetry employs suppressed syntax. Syntax, or something serving a similar function to syntax, is a very important feature of the best Imagist poetry. The term 'mosaic', which is sometimes used, is a bad one to apply to the assemblage of fragments which makes up a passage of Imagist verse, for each of the fragments carries with it the vestiges of the context, the structure, from which it has been torn—as a broken-off handle suggests the cup it belonged to.

Topaz I manage, and three sorts of blue;
but on the barb of time.
The fire? always, and the vision always,
Ear dull, perhaps, with the vision, flitting
And fading at will. Weaving with points of gold,
Gold-yellow, saffron . . .

When Hugh Kenner,† following Pound himself, compares writing of this kind to the springing of iron-filings into a rose-pattern at the approach of a magnet, the analogy, though powerful, is incomplete. For the 'filings' are already formed objects, fragments of absent sentences or dramas, gestures pointing in their own separate directions and reaching back towards their own origins. The ordering of these fragments

* See Donald Davie on 'Syntax as Music: Susanne Langer', in *Articulate Energy*, 1955, pp. 14–23.

† In *The Poetry of Ezra Pound*, 1951, *passim*.

into a 'rose-pattern' is only an achievement, and a feat of poetic strength, because the fragments themselves have a shape and will of their own; they are not inert 'filings' waiting to be magnetised, but a squad of disorderly troops, a congeries of squirming corpuscles. What makes 'H.D.' one of the few good Imagist poets apart from Pound is her command of strong, if 'suppressed', syntax. Her few fine poems are a taut chain of separate and arrested syntactical gestures, statements being interrupted by imperatives, and so on—a sort of ambiguous and 'ritual' syntax imitated and taken further by Eliot in *The Hollow Men.* I will quote 'Garden':

I

You are clear,
O rose, cut in rock
hard as the descent of hail.

I could scrape the colour
from the petals,
like spilt dye from a rock.

If I could break you
I could break a tree.

If I could stir
I could break a tree,
I could break you.

II

O wind,
rend open the heat,
cut apart the heat,
rend it to tatters.

Fruit cannot drop
through this thick air—
fruit cannot fall into heat
that presses up and blunts
the points of pears
and rounds the grapes.

Cut the heat—
plough through it,
turning it on either side
of your path.

Donald Davie seems to me wrong in talking of Imagist poetry, as he does in *Articulate Energy*, as if it were without syntax and employed spacing in place of it. He says:

> . . . if Landor was right in thinking that images in a poem must be 'spaced', then if the poet abandons the spacing he can get by syntax, he has to find some other means. Eliot and Pound find typography; the pause at the ends of lines or spaces in the middle of lines represent the interval which must be left by the reader between the impact of one image and the impact of another.[25]

But the only kind of 'images' which can be combined into a larger whole are ones which, at least potentially, form a whole in themselves. For clearly, if they were not to some extent self-sufficient—if they had no structure at all in themselves—it would make no sense to 'space' them. Since space (or time, which is what space signifies to a reader of print) is formless, though it can be measured, it can only constitute a relationship between things which have form.

As I have said, Pound gave a new and useful sense to the word 'image' when he used it to refer to a complete Imagist poem—the sense in which an entire *Noh* play can also be an 'image'. Used in this way, the word is suggestive, and not liable to be understood in any too-literal sense. I am less happy about the other kinds of meaning which he tried to make this hard-worked word bear (or the word 'phanopoeia', for which he exchanged it). Perhaps it was essential to his campaign for a neglected aspect of poetry; and he certainly used it subtly, and it helped to him some of his most creative insights. None the less, his thought became clearer when he adopted the notion of 'ideogram' and so took some of the burden off the word 'image'. For the word carries too much of a weight of paradox with it. The thing which a painter or sculptor produces—his painted canvas or sculpture—is an 'image' in a perfectly literal and everyday sense. It is something with an illusory resemblance to something else, whilst being made of different material. This is what we mean by calling an idol an 'image', and there is no puzzle about the word in this sense. A poet, however, doesn't produce anything of this sort. What a poet produces is a certain arrangement of words, which the reader has to repeat, a certain drill which he has to perform. It is as precise and determined and rigidly designed by the author as a painted or sculptured object, but it is obviously not an 'image' in this everyday sense of the word. The fact that in re-enacting its meaning the reader will form private mental images (different readers forming different ones) is bringing in the word 'image' in quite a different sense.

At all events, if you are going to accept the way Pound uses the word, with all its charge of metaphorical and polemical meaning, it is important to remember how much his use of it is coloured by his special talents and preoccupations as a poet —by his need to find common ground with post-impressionist artists, and his peculiar bent towards the phenomena, and metaphysics, of light.

3

THE WORDS TODAY

1 THE WORDS IN USE

Pound, though he later abandoned the term 'image', left an indelible mark on the word. His influence had the effect of aggrandising it generally, so that it has now taken over the role that 'imagination' had for the Romantics. The words 'image' and 'imagery' have grown bloated with the flesh of their rivals. They are words which writers and critics alike now feel they must bring in to any discussion of poetry—and, indeed, of fiction too. When Degas complained to Mallarmé: 'I've wasted a whole day on a damned sonnet, and haven't got an inch further, and yet it's not as if I didn't have ideas . . .', Mallarmé, as we know, replied; 'You don't make poems out of ideas. You make them out of words.' The instinctive present-day answer, I think, would be that you make them out of 'images'.

And this does not work altogether for good. The legacy which Pound left has been an awkward one; its effect on literary criticism generally, so it sometimes seems, has been to put the clock back, not forward. For it has been the great achievement of modern criticism to establish the rule that you cannot split works of art up, you may not separate form from content or discuss one aspect of form in isolation from all the others. And the discovery of 'imagery' has tended to undo all this and repeal this iron, uncomfortable law. Here, once again, is a feature, conveniently hybrid—neither exactly 'form' nor exactly 'content'; the missing link, or pineal gland connecting soul and body—which you *can* apparently isolate in the old happy way. With decent provisos, you can draw a circle round it and analyse it and docket it as something in its own right. Accordingly there has been a torrent of books on the 'imagery' of Marlowe, and Wordworth, and Proust. A school text of a Shakespeare play will have a separate little section on its 'imagery', as in the old days it would have had one on its 'characters', or earlier still on its 'immortal sayings'. The whole flavour of the new interest in 'imagery' is neo-Victorian and marks a step backwards in literary criticism.

I have already talked about Caroline Spurgeon and her *Shakespeare's Imagery and What It Tells Us*, in the course of arguing that it does, sometimes and somewhat, matter a little how you define 'imagery'. But the main point to make about her book, of course, is not simply one about definitions but about what she was trying to do. It is that, fundamentally, at least in the first part of her book, her interest in Shakespeare was biographical. She was studying Shakespeare's 'imagery' as you might study his handwriting or his portraits. And nothing wrong in that—only it hasn't much to do with literary criticism. The discoveries that she made—for instance that Shakespeare liked certain things for dinner and not others, or that he became more interested in sickness and medicine in middle age—were much the same as biographers use, to prove that Shakespeare was once a schoolmaster or went to sea or was Francis Bacon. Whatever they prove about Shakespeare the man, they tell us nothing about his work. Viewed as literary criticism, her programme of catching Shakespeare unawares and casting light on him by tracing the workings of his unconscious mind, amounted to a systematic ignoring of his art—in which he shows his mastery—in favour of the circumstances in regard to which he is helpless.

I don't want to suggest nothing good is to be got out of Caroline Spurgeon's book. She had some brilliant insights, especially in the second half of her book: on 'The Function of the Imagery as Background and Undertone in Shakespeare's Art'—for instance her famous observation that, throughout the play, Macbeth is seen as man dressed in clothes too big for him. And I think this may be a kind of insight which comes from looking at the play in a new—un-Bradleyan and un-Coleridgian—way. The novelty in her concept of 'iterated imagery' lay in noticing that something we were familiar with in poems could have an important role in plays as well—at least in Shakespeare's mature drama. Obviously no-one would be surprised to hear that Marvell, in *Upon Appleton House*, constantly iterates the idea of flowers as being like soldiers and gardens as resembling a battlefield—for that is the *raison d'être* of the poem. On the other hand, the core or *raison d'être* of a play, we are accustomed to think, is human action not a conceit or an expanded simile. And if characters in a play use figurative language—well, so they do in real life. There are plenty of 'dramatic' purposes this could serve, without our having to assume that it has thematic significance too. By noticing that it does so, Caroline Spurgeon enlarged our idea of what the word 'dramatic' can mean.

But if she pointed out a new feature in Shakespeare's plays, there was something basically wrong with the way she wanted us to interpret it. The trouble was there already in the title of this part of her book: 'The Function of Imagery as Background and Undertone . . .', and again in her opening remarks (p. 259) about the 'imagery' of the Comedies:

> As far as there is any continuous symbolism in the imagery of the comedies, its functions would seem to be . . . to give atmosphere and background, as well as to emphasise or re-echo certain qualities in the plays.

For, first of all, I don't think there can be anything called 'background' in a work of literature, considering it purely *as* a work of literature rather than as a representation of something. It sounds as if it were meant to be less important than the 'foreground'; and in a work of art, considered as such, nothing is more important than anything else, any more than the stalk of a plant is more 'important' than its leaves or petals. This is the implication of regarding works of art as 'organic wholes', a doctrine that critics are sometimes not very keen to follow to its full consequences.

Of course, if you are thinking of plays, there *is* something connected with them which you might reasonably call 'background'—I mean, painted scenery. But the point about scenery, obviously, is that it isn't an integral part of the play, and it wouldn't fundamentally matter if you had different scenery or none. A figurative allusion in a Shakespeare play is before anything else a part of a passage of verse or prose, in which all sorts of other things—metrical, tonal, architectonic, scenic, psychological—are going on at the same time; and each of these things not only acts on all the others, but is acted on by them. Whereas it is the fate of scenery to create an effect but to receive none back. Only one thing can justify thinking of the figurative language in a Shakespeare play as 'background' or as being like stage-scenery, and that is the argument that it works unconsciously. And this is just what Caroline Spurgeon holds (pp. 334–5):

> Enough has been said, I think, to indicate how complex and varied is the symbolism in the imagery of *Macbeth*, and to make it clear that an appreciable part of the emotions we feel throughout of pity, fear and horror, is due to the subtle but definite and repeated action of this imagery upon our minds, of which, in our preoccupation with the main theme, we remain largely unconscious.

But consider what this entails. If the effect of Shakespeare's 'iterative imagery' is unconscious, then it will not be an integral part of the experiencing of each line or passage as an aesthetic whole. It will be a separate strand in the evening's experience—like the noise of traffic from the street outside, or a private worry, except that it has a *general* relevance to the play in hand. What it would most resemble is Muzak, or the sort of 'subliminal' music you get in bad films.

And if you are ready to regard an element in a Shakespeare play as 'atmospheric' or Muzak-like, then it's quite sensible to discuss this element in mathematical terms—to count up the forty-two 'food, taste or cooking' images in *Troilus and Cressida*, and so on. For if each 'image' is thought of mainly as contributing to a sum of 'atmosphere', then arithmetic will be a main consideration. But what a view to take of the structure of a *Lear* or *Macbeth!*

Not long after the publication of *Shakespeare's Imagery*, a critic of the Spurgeon school, M. A. Rugoff, applied much the same method to Donne. And Rugoff staked out even larger claims for the method. Critics up to now, he says, have failed to realise what a rich mine of evidence is offered to them in a poet's 'imagery':

> Of the many ways in which the creative imagination of great writers has been approached, the most slighted, I think, is that of imagery . . . it has generally been treated by rhetoricians as one more technical adjunct of style, another of the handmaids of direct statement . . .
>
> All this has a place and serves a purpose, but what it

> has almost completely obscured is the fact that an image is, in its content, one of the freest of the imaginative contributions that a writer may make to a given statement of meaning. Although the meaning he is trying to convey may give the aim and purpose of the image, it will have no control over its substance and source; these the writer fixes upon almost at will. Because the image need meet the meaning of the passage only by way of analogy or illustration, the writer is left virtually untrammeled in his imaginative decision as to what its contents shall be. His fancy is given free rein—the wonderful liberty of developing a parallel or analogy out of anything from heaven, earth or the infinite world of the mind. Given such freedom, he turns naturally and inevitably to those things which, for reasons that lie as deep as personality itself, he has found most interesting, most vivid, most memorable. And in that exercise of choice, that almost arbitrary decision concerning what branch of learning or phase of life he will draw his image from—when, of course, that choice is repeated often enough or when it becomes part of a pattern—we get the most revelatory kinds of glimpses into the natural tides, drifts, and currents of a writer's creative imagination.[1]

And the 'freedom' for the imagination praised here is equivalent to unconsciousness. The writer's greatness comes out in the things he does without knowing he is doing them:

> One of the most interesting things about the content of images is that their disclosures are, in a sense, almost unwitting . . . The remarkable thing, then, is that although the image is a finished product of his art, the writer remains virtually unaware of what its contents, when studied along with thousands of others from his pen, may reveal.[2]

Further, a writer's 'imagery' contains the essence of his writing—with the implication that the rest of his work is only a sort of neutral vehicle or necessary base matter, or perhaps a gaoler to be outwitted.

> Where his [Donne's] obligation to a patron or his position as a priest in the Church of England may well have dictated the actual theme and substance respectively of a eulogistic poem and an Easter Day sermon, the figures of speech which

he introduces into such pieces are virtually uncontrolled
by extraneous considerations and embody pure imagination.[3]

But I think it's clear enough that the aim prescribed for the critic by Rugoff, as by Caroline Spurgeon, is really a kind of biography. 'Imagery' will help him to study, not Donne's actual work, but his 'creative imagination'—about which you can find evidence (revelations indeed) in his 'imagery', as the detective finds evidence in cigarette-ash and bus-tickets. The 'creative imagination' or 'pure imagination' is an autonomous force, a free operator, able to function regardless of circumstances. It does not operate upon its surroundings; it turns its back on them in proud self-sufficiency. It is the private enemy of the 'official' poem—which it would, if it could, destroy. Like a prisoner in the Bastille, the poet—the unconscious possessor of 'pure imagination'—asserts his freedom only in his dreams.

I really think it is not possible to regard literature in this way—and for several reasons. For, first of all, 'pure imagination' —even allowing for this being a playful phrase—surely must be a chimera? The imagination can only be revealed, indeed can only exist, in the effect it has *on* something. It doesn't conduct an autonomous existence, like a god in the head; and if it did, and you even managed to interview it there, it could still tell you nothing about poems.

Again, it is returning to a darker age of criticism to identify some feature of a literary work as its 'essence' and the rest as its vehicle. And that is what you are doing, if, by a false extrapolation from Imagist poetry, you regard the 'images' in Shakespeare or Donne as little poems-within-a-poem; for this leaves the rest of the poem as so much rubble or base metal and implies that the critic, by concentrating on the 'images' (the essence or pure ore of the poem) can bring to light the real, the essential, work of art hidden from both the unenlightened reader and from the author himself. The author, at the mercy of his unconscious associations, is not aware that he is producing this work-within-a-work, whereas it is revealed to the critic—partly by simple arithmetic, the simple process of counting the author's 'image-clusters' and verbal repetitions.

This leads on to a third objection, that scrutinising 'imagery' in this way goes with regarding the writer as a naif genius or holy idiot, performing his best and most complex feats in a condition of inspired stupor—and this is to put the clock of criticism back even further, coming near to calling Shakespeare fancy's child, warbling his native woodnotes wild. It violates a principle I would regard as self-evident, which is that a writer, or at least a good writer, always knows *what* he is doing, even if he doesn't know why he is doing it, or what he has done when he has done it. He may not be conscious (indeed he cannot be fully conscious) of the sources of his work, and he may not understand its meaning when he has produced it (as Eliot always claimed to keep an open mind towards other people's interpretations of his poems), but he is fully conscious of his own art. He knows he must lay an emphasis *here*, and form a connection *there*, and he has, better than any critic, a living sense of the whole work in its relation to its parts.

All these objections, and especially the last, apply again to Robert Heilman, when he writes as follows during a discussion of *Othello*:

> One might speak of an image-system as an inner organism —a part of the whole that could not exist without the whole and yet an entity having parts that function with respect to each other. This would be a 'verbal drama' as distinct from 'verbal drama' generally. As a created thing it does not 'just happen'; nor yet, I believe, is it deliberately blue-printed and executed. One may surmise: a certain image or kind of image 'comes up' for a speaker on a certain occasion; then it is felt consciously or semi-consciously to have some relevance to the import of the whole; and it continues to be used (with the varying degrees of consciousness presumably characteristic of the creative process) as a way of exploring character or mood or theme during the constructive process and leaving a trail by which the reader may follow the exploration in the finished work.[4]

It is the phrase 'varying degrees of consciousness' which is suspicious. To make the existence of his 'image-system' plausible, Heilman has to admit that Shakespeare himself might only have been 'semi-conscious' of it, it being the habit of writers to compose in a state of absorbed inattention. There is something slighting to Shakespeare in this. For an 'image-system' sounds as if it must be an important structural element in a play, and an author could not afford not to be conscious, and not just 'semi-conscious', of anything so fundamental.*

But if this is slighting to Shakespeare he suffers even more indignity from another line of argument, fostered by using the words 'image' and 'imagery' in place of 'metaphor' and 'simile'. I mean the way of talking which degrades (or elevates) metaphor into a relic of pre-rational thinking—something not on a level with the other activities an author engages in, but at once below and above them, more primitive and more ineffable. Here is Paul Haeffner:

> Imagery is a form of metaphor or figurative speech, a kind of picture language. Shakespeare and his audience rarely thought literally and a rational argument was to them only half an argument. They had to be able to see and feel it with their imagination and their senses. By expressing himself through images, Shakespeare could be more certain of involving his listeners more completely; but imagery was also a way of showing, through poetry (as it always has been), how all things in life and the universe are related; the poet can tell us more about his subject or theme by interpreting them in terms of something else. In this way, too, he can put us in touch with the mysteries of existence as he sees them.[5]

There is something very paradoxical about this. It amounts to saying that Shakespeare, in metaphorical passages, far from showing his supreme mastery of language, is actually turning his back on verbal language. Out of tenderness for his audience's (and apparently his own) limitations he is resorting to picture-language instead. The high intellectual activity of a mind, putting out all its force to strain language to its ends, is reduced to a kind of dumb-show manipulating the 'senses'.

In the years following the publication of Caroline Spurgeon's pioneer study, a number of critics attacked her methods. Rosemond Tuve made some of the essential objections in an Appendix to her *Elizabethan and Metaphysical Imagery*, 1947, pp. 422–3.

* Oscar J. Campbell attacks the notion of 'image-systems' in Shakespeare, though not in a way I find very sympathetic, in his swingeing 'Shakespeare and the "New" Critics' (*Joseph Quincy Adams: Memorial Studies*, ed. J. G. McManaway *et. al.*, 1948, p. 93 *et seq.*). He was answered by L. C. Knights in *Some Shakespearian Themes* (1959).

Recent studies of imagery have used almost entirely as a basis for characterising and grouping images: the *kind* of *content* whence authors draw (1) descriptive detail and (2) second terms (things compared to, vehicles) of images. In the first place, 1 and 2 represent very different mental operations, differently caused. In the second place, the factor chiefly regarded in the drawing of conclusions is the author's predilection for certain contents. The number of other factors involved—and impossible to isolate—in the creation of choice of even the simplest image seems to me to throw this method out of court; . . .

One initial difficulty any reader may test for himself. It is seldom possible to determine except by an arbitrary decision the province to which an image's content allows us to assign it. . . . Even objects are unsafe; for Marlowe, 'brass vessels' may belong to the province of commonplace domestic objects, for me, to whatever province would include art museums in a remote and 'romantic' foreign country—and no reader of either of our images could ever tell it. Let the image mention not objects but things historical, religious or political, and one is in far worse case. No NED could tell us the precise overtones of a particular 'vehicle' to a certain man in a certain region in a certain year, and our knowledge of social and political currents would have to be unimaginably delicate. But suppose we could surmount these difficulties.

We should yet have images ranged according to a basis of 'likeness' which is almost completely irrelevant *to the effect of the image as an element of aesthetic form.* All that is poetically important about the image is yet undetermined. The best test of this is to try it with a few poems and notice what strange bedfellows any image must receive. Marlowe's brass-vessels image, for example, must range itself with St. Teresa's cup of death in Crashaw. I do not know anything that could be less illuminating to the critic of the two poems.

Moreover, images do not start and stop, in poems. They merge, are indistinguishable from the offspring they beget, refuse to be separated from a matrix of conceptual statement, and often turn out to be coterminous with the whole poem. It is often quite impossible to count the number of images in a

> poem; the number will differ *for the same reader* in different readings. We can frequently be entirely certain that an author is using language tropically; there are other cases where we do not know and can never find out.

And in *The Development of Shakespeare's Imagery* (1951), Wolfgang Clemen took up the challenge. Caroline Spurgeon had studied the content of Shakespeare's 'images'; he proposed to study their form, and their relationship to their dramatic context. It sounds a much more promising approach. However, the result was not quite what you would expect; and not as different from Caroline Spurgeon's as you might have hoped.

Once again, I shall have to tackle his book with a sort of mad pedantry. For it does seem to drive one back on asking what is actually meant by 'images' and 'imagery'. The kind of thing that Clemen has in mind, when he speaks of the relationship of 'imagery' to its dramatic context, is the way in which the 'images' in Salarino's speeches to Antonio in the first scene of *The Merchant of Venice* foreshadow future events. If I were a merchant, says Salarino,

> My wind cooling my broth
> Would blow me to an ague, when I thought
> What harm a wind too great at sea might do.
> I should not see the sandy hour-glass run
> But I should think of shallows and of flats,
> And see my wealthy Andrew dock'd in sand
> Veiling her high-top lower than her ribs
> To kiss her burial.
>
> (1.i.22)

'Here Shakespeare's art of dramatic irony becomes manifest,' remarks Clemen.

> Salarino—first thinking of his breath with which he cools his soup—imagines what would probably happen if a storm should strike the ships on the high seas. This is spoken in passing, the picture is half-playfully executed, almost for its own sake . . . But these few seconds have sufficed for Shakespeare to attain his aim; the audience has pricked up its ears; upon the imagination a very definite image has impressed itself for a brief moment, and this will come to life again later on when reality demands it.[6]

Here we are up against the queer sort of puzzle that arises when people talk about 'images'. Because, where are the 'images'? Not in the metaphors, surely? Salarino says, perfectly literally, that if he were Antonio, when he blew on his soup it would put him in mind of high winds at sea. Admittedly, this putting in mind would have been occasioned by analogy; but no metaphor is in question. Salarino certainly uses metaphors—ones about being 'blown into an ague' and about a sinking ship 'kissing its burial'; but if the passage is prophetic of later events in the play, it is not because of its metaphors about agues and burials.

As with so many critics, Clemen's definition of 'imagery' is extraordinarily slippery and elusive. A good deal of the time he talks as if 'images' were much the same thing as metaphors. But as he uses the word here, he seems to mean something quite different—i.e. a passage in which someone, not the author, is conjuring up an imaginary scene. It is a meaning he uses again when he refers to the mad Lear's imaginings (when Lear pictures to himself a beadle whipping a whore, or the wren and the 'small gilded fly' copulating in his sight) as 'imagery'. And elsewhere he talks of occasions when an 'image' appears 'in the guise of' comparison, simile, personification, metaphor or metonymy; and again of 'images' being 'prepared for' by metaphorical language (p. 221); which again implies that 'imagery' is a different sort of thing from metaphors: not metaphor, but the fruit of metaphor. And not only can you have 'images' which don't contain a metaphor, you can actually have 'images' which *do* contain metaphors (like the metaphors of 'blowing into an ague' and ships kissing their burial) and yet the metaphors have nothing to do with their being 'images'. Thus he speaks of Cassio's lines about Desdemona's miraculous rescue after her stormy voyage as 'sea-imagery' (p. 96)—whereas if metaphors were the point, you would have to call this 'traitor-imagery' or 'political imagery'.

But if a character conjuring up an absent scene is 'imagery', where do you stop? Presumably Jacques's picture of the seven ages of man is 'imagery'—for we don't actually see the puling infant and the unwilling schoolboy on the stage. And then perhaps any *messenger's* speech . . .

Of course there are words which are perfectly vague and quite impossible to define rigidly and yet are useful to critics—

like the word 'vulgarity'. But then they are emotive words: they don't refer to a technical feature. The trouble with 'imagery' is that it appears to refer to some technical feature in literature—like 'rhythm' or 'stanza' or 'metaphor'—yet it is hard to discover *what.* And one can see how writing a book about such a vague phenomenon leads Clemen to invoke an even vaguer one, 'atmosphere' (the vaguest of all literary terms except perhaps 'world', and from the same cosmological vocabulary).* I have often sympathised with schoolboys who, when asked to write about 'Dickens's use of atmosphere', think it must mean all that fog in *Bleak House.* For though it is a convenient *façon de parler* to talk about the 'atmosphere' in works of literature—say, the atmosphere of blackness and disrupted Nature in *Macbeth*—or the 'atmosphere' surrounding certain literary characters—'Othello brings with him the magic spell of distant lands and exotic things'—it is really only the language of casual conversation. It is the way you would talk when you wanted to allude to something without bothering to imagine it precisely. You remember the 'atmosphere' of a book as you might remember the binding of the copy you read it in. The word is good enough to describe your own general, unfocused recollections of a work of art, but it is a hopeless one to apply to artistic effects themselves. You can't seriously talk of Shakespeare writing the first scene of *Hamlet* to 'create atmosphere'—that is the language of Grub Street. The scene exists for its own sake, and is a complex work of art, with an elaborate structure of its own, forming part of a larger structure. Keats's *Odes,* when you think of them casually, each seems to have its special 'atmosphere'—but when you start to think what you mean by this, you find you simply mean the whole poem and everything about it. 'Atmosphere' is a useless word to apply to works of art because it suggests something formless and fuzzy, whereas works of art are, through and through, things of form and structure.

Thus when Clemen discusses what, according to him, is one of the main functions of 'imagery' in Shakespeare—that it creates, or adds to, the 'atmosphere' of a play—he implies an idea of the play, or this aspect of it, as mere formless accumulation. For instance, when he writes of a passage from *Julius Caesar:*

* See Chapter 5, pp. 113–124.

In the third scene the conspirators meet in the streets of Rome at night during a terrific thunderstorm. By means of this imagery, the night and the thunderstorm are made very vivid, being also a suitable background for the dark conspiracy. The mood and situation naturally suggest the likening of Caesar to this fearful night.

CASSIUS: Now could I, Casca, name to thee a man
Most like this dreadful night,
That thunders, lightens, opens graves, and roars
As doth the lion in the Capitol, (1.iii.72)

The image fulfils two functions at one and the same time, it characterises Caesar, and adds to the nocturnal thunderstorm atmosphere.[7]

As if Shakespeare's art in this scene consisted in slipping in as many allusions to nocturnal thunderstorms as he could. This is the naive mathematical approach which the words 'imagery' and 'atmosphere' both encourage. It is there again when Clemen says: 'We all of us are aware of the strong earthy atmosphere pervading the play. Except for *A Midsummer Night's Dream* and *King Lear* there is no other play of Shakespeare's in which so many plants, fruits and animals appear.' And it leads logically to admitting that what you are doing in studying and cataloguing the 'imagery' in Shakespeare's plays is merely finding confirmation for something you knew already.

The imagery in *Cymbeline*, seen from this point of view, thus again confirms the general impression which we receive when reading the play.[8]

Writing about 'imagery' and writing about 'atmosphere' both turn out to be acts of supererogation.

Clemen's pages also hint at another doctrine, which is that 'imagery' is somehow *truth-telling*—you can trust the 'imagery', as opposed to any other element in the play, to tell you what Shakespeare really thought. Certainly, Clemen sees dangers in this doctrine; yet with careful provisos, he believes it to be true.

In the chapter on *Coriolanus* the question was raised to what degree we are justified in drawing from the

> imagery conclusions as to Shakespeare's own views and his personal likes and dislikes. While it was in general thought right to approach this problem with the utmost reserve and caution, *Coriolanus* seemed to provide an exception to the rule. The lavish and outspoken use of images and the depreciatory names for the 'rabble' seemed to indicate a strong antipathy on the part of Shakespeare to this class of people, especially as this was brought out by other plays as well.[9]

This seems to be merely a refinement of Caroline Spurgeon's 'detective' approach—part of a scheme for taking the author, or the play, by surprise, by scrutinising clues and 'evidence'. And it belongs with the general tendency I have mentioned already, to give 'imagery' a special status—more naive, more exalted, and less conscious than the other elements in the plays; as if the rest of the play were a sort of base matter and the 'imagery' were its 'soul-life'. This surely is a discredited way of looking at works of literature. Critics such as Clemen, writing after Eliot, would be very down on a dramatist like Shaw, who makes his characters voice his own philosophy of life. Yet voicing it through 'imagery', or any other single feature of a work of literature, seems just as bad; and the fact that the author is doing it unconsciously doesn't make it any better. If Shakespeare's views come through directly, then to that extent he must be creating an inferior kind of art. The right view is surely Eliot's, in his essay 'The Possibility of a Poetic Drama', when he says that an idea can remain pure in a work of art only if 'It has become so identified with the reality that you can no longer say what the idea is.'

Yet another kind of trouble fostered by these greedy and confusing words 'image' and 'imagery' can be seen in Rosemond Tuve's own *Elizabethan and Metaphysical Imagery*. The purpose of her book was to jolt us out of our modern prejudices about poetry and put us in the way of enjoying aspects of Elizabethan verse these have blinded us to. Brought up on Eliot and the Imagists, she argues, we have certain narrow expectations of poetry: we expect it to present either simple sense-experiences, or, at most, a state of mind communicated by a selection of sense-impressions. We demand that verse should be 'sensuous', and we object to all discursive and general statement in it. Now Elizabethan verse, she says, is sometimes full of richly sensuous 'imagery', which taken by itself is similar to what you find in Keats and Amy Lowell. But even when this is so, the 'images' perform a very different function: they are immediately harnessed to the service of some rational and general proposition. And very often, she says, its 'imagery' is not sensuous at all, but purely general and abstract (for instance in most Elizabethan songs); and this makes the modern reader uncomfortable—so that, increasingly, he turns away from the Elizabethans to the Jacobean and metaphysical poets, who are more like what he knows.

But the truth is, she says, we are too blinkered by recent conceptions of poetry to enter into the Elizabethan poetic, with its roots in formal logic and rhetoric.

> Our suspicion is waked when we find that the Elizabethan was not generally writing (rarely even for the length of a single image) 'here is the thing that happened, here the object, the landscape, the human being that was seen'. It still more wakes our suspicions to notice that he was not generally writing 'this is how *I* felt about the experience, how *I* saw the object, the landscape'.[10]

We are prevented by 'the peculiar modern humility (arrogant enough) which thirsts for presentations of the whole baffling, ironic, conflict-filled complex of life'—by our 'avidity for the particular'—from appreciating a poetry based on the general.

Her book is an attack on the anachronisms of modern readers—and the trouble is that it suffers from the same kind of anachronism. For, first of all, as she admits herself, though part of the argument of her book is that if you are going to study Elizabethan poetry you had better pay serious attention to what Elizabethan critics said about it, the fact is that Renaissance poetic theorists didn't actually recognise a general feature of poetry called 'images'. 'It is not easy,' she says,

> to draw up a list of criteria for images in the Renaissance. They sit on no branch ready for plucking, for theorists do not isolate 'images' as an element in poetic technique . . . [11]

But then, her book makes you wonder if anyone should do so. For there is a basic muddle in her way of using the word. In one place she will talk about 'images' as though the word meant 'picture', so that she speaks of the 'images' in Eliot's lines:

The winter evening settles down
With smell of steaks in passageways.
Six o'clock.
The burnt-out ends of smoky days.
And now a gusty shower wraps
The grimy scraps
Of withered leaves about your feet
And newspapers from vacant lots . . .

But in another place she will use the word as if it meant 'comparisons' and refers to Marlowe's far-fetched one in *Hero and Leander*:

. . . Nature wept, thinking she was undone,
Because she took more from her than she left,
And of such wondrous beauty her bereft:
Therefore, in sign her treasure suffer'd wrack,
Since Hero's time hath half the world been black.

as an 'image'; or again this quatrain from Donne:

Thou art not soft, and cleare, and strait, and faire,
As *Down*, as *Stars*, *Cedars*, and *Lillies* are,
But thy right hand, and cheek, and eye, only
Are like thy other hand, and cheek, and eye.

And since the Eliot lines are not a comparison, and the Marlowe and Donne passages are not pictures, it seems as if she were using the word 'image' in two quite unrelated senses. Thus her whole basis for comparing post-Symbolist verse and Elizabethan verse seems, at least here, to be non-existent—just a confusion bred by an ambiguous word.

It would be stupid to score a pedantic victory over Rosemond Tuve. Her *Elizabethan and Metaphysical Imagery* is an impressive book and opens up a vast subject (the whole influence of rhetorical and logical training on Elizabethan poets). It would be absurd to talk as if her book were useless; no-one could fail to learn about Elizabethan poetry from it, or to see it in a new light.—Yet there is an important sense in which her book *is* useless. She tells us invaluable facts, but her theory as to how one should actually read and respond to Elizabethan verse doesn't work at all. Consider her account, in terms of rhetorical technique, of a passage in *Hero and Leander*:

> . . . these are still just examples of the small rhetorical *fictio* used to praise. . . . The images which impress us with Leander's beauty are similarly constructed and similar in tone. Then comes a passage, the description of Venus's temple, in which the images approach the very nearly nonlogical functions of a rhetorical *descriptio*. Accordingly, their terms are at first richly sensuous, coming as close as Elizabethan writers come to sensuous precision (the terms are still amplifications). As Marlowe approaches the first small climax in his narrative—Leander's falling in love at first sight—the images take on a further function; they begin to show in their form the character of images used to set a special emotional pitch. This shift is not necessarily highly deliberate; if it were, perhaps it would not show up with such consistency in so many authors of different eras and habits of mind. The heavy, full series of the voluptuous encounters with the gods (i, 143–56) has an effect chiefly upon mood, blotting out other aspects of reality with a recurrent drumbeat of amorousness, much as a tone-poem swathes hearers in a single mood. For the swiftly connotative allusions serve a function frequently served by images in modern poetry, approximating the effect of insistently repeated motifs in certain types of music (usually program music).[12]

As a critical analysis, especially in its fearful musical excursions, it is pretty impossible. What's wrong with it is not just the mixture of pedantry and lushness in the style. It is that Rosemond Tuve's whole taste, her general sense of artistic values and relevant comparisons, are too shaky. And thus her accusation anachronism in modern readers of Elizabethan poetry rebounds on her. The weakness in her book lies not in the differences she sees between Elizabethan and modern verse, but in the likenesses. Could anyone seriously consider, as she does, that these lines from *Hero and Leander*

Far from the town (where all is whist and still,
Save that the sea, playing on yellow sand,
Sends forth a rattling murmur to the land
Whose sound allures the golden Morpheus
In silence of the night to visit us)
My turret stands . . .

are like Keats? It seems obvious that in writing 'Sends forth a rattling murmur to the land', Marlowe isn't being 'sensuous' in a Keatsian sense at all—he is not trying to evoke a particular sound or experience in Nature (or if he is, he is making a very bad job of it). Nor, again, though she suggests so, is there anything 'particularised', or in the least like Amy Lowell and the Imagists, in Ben Jonson's charming lines:

Ha' you felt the wooll of Bever?
Or Swans Downe ever?
Or have smelt o' the bud o' the Brier?
Or the Nard in the fire?
Or have tasted the bag of the bee?
O so white! O so soft! O so sweet is she!

They don't attempt to tell you what kind of whiteness or softness 'she' possessed.

Even odder is the parallel and contrast she makes between Donne's *Elegy XI. Upon the losse of his Mistresses Chaine, for which he made satisfaction* and Eliot's *Prufrock*. The difference, she says, is that

> Eliot shows us a man having a thought. Donne arranges the thoughts a man had, upon losing his mistress' property, into a carefully logical and hence wantonly witty exposition of the 'bitter' and disproportionate cost of ladies.
>
> The measure of the difference is the strict logical coherence of Donne's images. This does not mean that the images are not sensuously vivid; only that they are not primarily so. Each is chosen and presented as a 'significant' part of an ordered pattern, and every care is taken to make that order rationally apprehensible. The relation of each image to the point in hand is as clear, to us, as logical association can make it—the relation of circumcis'd French crowns and unlickt Spanish bear-whelps to bad money, the

relation of martyred angels in the fire to wasted good money.[13]

What is puzzling here is why she should speak of Donne's 'images' in the passage as 'sensuously vivid'. What is there 'sensuous' about likening money to circumcis'd crowns and unlickt Spanish bear-whelps? Donne writes:

> O, shall twelve righteous Angels, which as yet
> No leaven of vile soder did admit;
> . . . Shall they be damn'd and in the furnace throwne,
> And punisht for offences not their owne?
> They save not me, they doe not ease my paines,
> When in that hell they'are burnt and tyed in chains.
> Were they but Crownes of France, I cared not,
> For, most of these, their naturall Countreys rot
> I think possesseth, they come hear to us,
> So pale, so lame, so leane, so ruinous;
> And howso'er French kings most Christian be,
> Their Crownes are circumcis'd most Jewishly.
> Or were they Spanish Stamps, still travelling.
> That are become as Catholique as their King,
> Those unlickt beare-whelps, unfil'd pistolets
> That more than Canon shot availes or lets;
> . . . if thou love let them alone,
> For thou will love me lesse when they are gone;
> And be content that some lowd squeaking Cryer
> Well-pleas'd with one leane thred-bare groat, for hire,
> May like a devill roare through every street;
> And gall the finders concience, if they meet.

And the comparisons, so far as one can see, are purely logical—an elaborate punning conceit on clipped coins and venereal disease and a play on the shapelessness of Spanish coins and the (proverbial) shapelessness of new-born bears (until licked into shape by their mothers). They are 'vivid' because they show Donne's mind in a hurry of imaginative activity, not because there is anything 'sensuous' about them.

However, this is a puzzle that often arises when people talk about 'images' and 'imagery'. They speak as though, because a thing has to be perceived by the senses—as everything in the material universe has to be—its appearance in a metaphor makes the metaphor 'sensuous'. It is a good example of the seductions of the word 'imagery'. No normal person thinks of courts of law, or legal briefs, or lawyers' fees as being 'sensuous', but as soon as they turn up in a metaphor (as they might do, say, in a sonnet by Shakespeare) and so can be called 'legal imagery', the strange idea that they are 'sensuous' somehow creeps in. The result is to leave you with no word to describe what poets like Keats and Hopkins are doing when they are deliberately evoking physical feelings and the life of the senses.

Rosemond Tuve's remarks about the *Prufrock* side of the comparison are equally queer.

> Eliot's 'lonely men in shirt-sleeves, leaning out of windows' are no less clearly seen than Donne's 'lowd squeaking Cryer'*; but their attachment to their author's meaning is; for Donne's crier is a perspicuously logical part of his suggestion that the lady might save more than money by letting him out of the restitution.[14]

She doesn't mention the dramatic point of Prufrock's 'lonely men in short sleeves', which is that Prufrock *knows* they are quite irrelevant. If he were to talk about them, it would be a way of *not* saying what he meant—for what he really has to say is something incommunicable. Thus their 'attachment to their author's meaning, is extremely clear and logical.

But if this comparison of Rosemond Tuve's is inept, I have a feeling that she would never have thought of making it if it hadn't been for the concept called 'imagery' and the muddles it brings in its train. And, in general, there seems something illogical in saying that, in order to discuss Renaissance poets, you need the old terms of Renaissance rhetoric, and then imposing a quite new one on them—the 'image'; and not only that, but elaborating it, in pastiche Puttenham style, into the 'conical image', the 'radical image', etc.—almost as bad as Puttenham's own *Sillespis*, *Hypozeuxis* and *Aposiopesis* and the rest of the hideous crew.

2 ATTEMPTS AT DEFINITION

The general run of modern critics tend to take the words

* It is perhaps worth pointing out that there is something 'sensuously vivid' about *this* phrase of Donne's.

'image' and 'imagery' as if they needed no defining. And understandably enough, because disputes about definitions can be pretty tedious. Still it wouldn't be too unfair to say of them, as T. H. Pear does in the *Encyclopaedia Britannica*,

> one may open a book on, for example, Shakespeare's imagery, without knowing if the writer is concerned with the poet's use of figures of speech, his power of suggesting imagery to the reader by descriptive writing, whether figurative or not, or the imagery (visual, auditory, kinesthetic, etc.) which the poet himself experiences . . .

And when critics do try to define the term 'image' rigorously, they tend to find they have, not a meaning, but a family of meanings, on their hands. For instance, C. Day Lewis, in defining the word in *The Poetic Image*, gives two quite different explanations in the same sentence.

> What do we understand, then, by the poetic image? In its simplest terms, it is a picture made out of words. An epithet, a metaphor, a simile may create an image; or an image may be presented to us in a phrase or passage on the face of it purely descriptive, but conveying to our imagination something more than the accurate reflection of an external reality.[15]

However, at least two critics, Middleton Murry and Hugh Kenner, have made really serious and sustained efforts at defining the word and staking out a claim for it as an improved synonym for 'metaphor'.

Murry begins with the warning that discussing metaphor at all is a worrying business, since the very language you use to discuss it in is metaphorical. At every moment you find yourself faced with infinite recessions.

> . . . the investigation of metaphor is curiously like the investigation of any of the primary data of consciousness: it cannot be pursued very far without our being led to the borderline of sanity.[16]

He chooses therefore to ignore the dead or dormant metaphors of which all our speech is composed, and to consider only the 'present, hazardous, incomplete and thrilling exploration of reality' found in the metaphors of creative literature. Does it make any difference in speaking of them, he asks, whether we use the terms 'metaphor' and 'simile', or the term 'image'? Well, the distinction between 'metaphor' and 'simile' seems plainly to be only a formal one—metaphor, as Aristotle said, is compressed simile: the 'act of creative perception' is the same in either case. The word 'image' is more 'recalcitrant', however. It loses some of the sense of the word 'simile', and it tends to force the part played by the *visual* image too much into the foreground. (In Baudelaire's 'agonising' simile,

> Ces affreuses nuits
> Qui compriment le cœur comme un papier qu'on froisse

'the visual image has no part at all'.)

All the same, he concludes, the word 'image' is indispensable.

> For metaphor and simile belong to formal classification. The word 'image', precisely because it is used to cover both metaphor and simile, can be used to point towards their fundamental identity; and if we resolutely exclude from our minds the suggestion that the image is solely or even predominantly visual, and allow the word to share in the heightened and comprehensive significance with which its derivative 'imagination' has perforce been endowed—if we conceive the 'image' not as primary and independent, but as the most singular and potent instrument of the faculty of imagination—it is a more valuable word than those which it subsumes: metaphor and simile. To them cling something worse than false suggestion: a logical taint, an aura of irrelevancy.[17]

To think of metaphors and similes as 'figures of speech' is inadequate and misleading, he thinks, because metaphor, renamed 'the image', constitutes the fundamental creative act in literature. The metaphors of great writers 'make an advance in the conquest of some reality' and are felt to be 'the vehicle of some immediate revelation to those who attend to them'. The greatest mastery of imagery 'does not lie in the use, however beautiful and revealing, of isolated images, but in the harmonious total impression produced by a succession of subtly related images'; and such achievements 'are to be conceived as a swift and continuous act of exploration of the world of imagination'. Metaphor or 'imagery' is the heart of creative literature, for the good reason that literature, or at least great literature, explores a special 'world' or 'universe'— a 'universe of quality' (as opposed to the 'universe of quantity' known to physicists). It deals with a universe 'wherein quality leaps to cohere with quality across the abysms of classification that divide and categorise the universe of intellectual apprehension' and which has 'analogy for its most essential language'. The true citizens of this universe are the masters of metaphor, and 'the authentic messages they bring from that near yet distant country perplex our brains and comfort our souls with that half-assurance that the things that are may be otherwise than as we know them'.

It is an impressive essay, and especially in its repeated warnings that *all* this talk is metaphorical. Still, I think it plainly conveys a false notion of what literature is. And where it goes wrong is precisely in the step by which an essay that sets out to deal with 'metaphor' ends up as an essay on 'imagery'. For of course there is a sense in which all literature (poetic and prose fictions alike) is a 'metaphor' and an 'analogy'. Experiencing literature is 'like' living, in the sense in which two utterly different things can be like each other. One should remember that there are two senses of the word 'like'. The giant and the bearded lady at the fair are more 'like' each other, in the sense of having more in common, than the roses on wallpaper are like roses in the garden. But when we say that books are like life, or reading is like living, we mean it in the sense in which the roses on wallpaper are like the real ones. Literature is a purely voluntary and gratuitous activity, with nothing in common with the involuntary experience of living. (In literature it is no impossible paradox for Flaubert to say that he *is* Madame Bovary.) But in virtue of its extreme difference, literature can be made to stand as an analogy for life—a symbol or 'metaphor' for it. However, if you call literature a 'metaphor' in this sense, you are using the word 'metaphor' itself in a figurative sense, the same sense in which painting and sculpture are 'metaphors'. It is essential to distinguish this from the older technical sense of 'metaphor' as a verbal instrument or figure of speech—an instrument of huge potentiality in literature and which (as I argued in my opening pages) has no real counterpart in painting at all. By jettisoning the precise term 'metaphor' for the more grandiose term 'image', Murry is obscuring a fundamental difference between literature and the other arts.

Whatever may be the case with analogies in a magical or Hermetic views of the universe, or as they figure in dreams and the Unconscious, analogies in literature are never *just* analogies. They are also words in a certain order, producing dynamic effects through their logical associations, through their syntax, and through all sorts of rhythmic, acoustic and mimetic qualities—and all these things simultaneously. Middleton Murry, indeed, mentions Shakespeare's control of 'tempo and rhythm' and the 'characteristic swiftness of his language' in handling a sequence of metaphors. But these are only a beginning of the endless range of expressive means open to a poet. And when he talks about Shakespeare's *Antony and Cleopatra* in this essay, the impression he gives is of something static—not a complex activity, which the reader is being made to re-perform, but a map laid out, telling of a journey to some *terra incognita* of spiritual reality. The poet has 'charted' this region; he has done all the work. And when the reader has made use of his chart to guide him in his voyage to this transcendental 'region', 'world', 'universe', or 'near yet distant country', he can, you feel, cheerfully throw it away. The work of art itself is depreciated; all the value lies in the 'country' it gives him access to. It is a fundamentally utilitarian view of literature, which values it, not for what it is in itself, but for doing the work of revelation and prophecy.

An even more interesting and original attempt at defining an 'image', as something akin to a metaphor, was made by Hugh Kenner, in a student manual called *The Art of Poetry* (New York, 1959). Kenner says quite simply that an 'image' is 'what the words actually name'. In ninety-per-cent of the writing you encounter, he says, you are intended to ignore the literal sense of the words. The author means you to skate over a sentence like 'There exists a solid argument favouring such a course', making a guess at its probable meaning, and ignoring the fact that *course* (a motion from point to point); *favour* (to look upon with esteem); and *solid* (not hollow or soft) are notions which simply don't hang together, and would produce a sort of monster if you paused to realise their meaning. Half of Western education is devoted to teaching you the trick of this skating kind of reading, and it all has to be unlearned by anyone wanting to enjoy genuine writing—especially poetry. To read poems you have to learn to trust 'that the words mean what they say'.

And what the words say is very often the name of a *thing*. Words like 'solid' are borrowed from the language in which we describe material things. ('When Shakespeare writes "Night's candles are burnt out" you are to think of candles.') And poets, and good writers in general, following this hint provided by language itself, have found that their meaning can generally be best expressed by means of a *thing*. Thus when Confucius says

The proper man is not a dish.

he is, says Kenner, expressing something which he could never have expressed by abstract words, like 'The proper man is honest'. It is precise (unlike 'The proper man is honest', for a term like 'honest' can be stretched to mean anything a speaker chooses). And at the same time it is very rich: ' "Dish" *in this sentence* is . . . richer than any of the usual attributes of propriety.' It contains a whole range of implications such as

. . . is independent,
. . . is not a passive learner,
. . . is inexhaustible,
. . . is a giver, not a receiver, of wisdom,
. . . is not shallow,
and so on.

And it derives this richness of meaning not from the dictionary but from *being juxtaposed with* 'The proper man'. 'When words are skilfully put together (juxtaposed, literally put together, placed in contact) they generate potentials of this kind; exactly as, when you touch electric terminals together, you get a spark.' *Dish* in this example, says Kenner, 'may be called an *image*: a thing the writer names and introduces because its presence in the piece of writing will release and clarify meaning'.

For Kenner, the attraction of defining an 'image' in this way—'The image is what the words actually name'—is clearly that it sidesteps the belittling notion of an 'image' as a device or figure of speech; it makes it something almost as basic as language, or naming, itself. What's wrong with the terms for figures of speech, like 'metaphor' or 'simile' or 'synecdoche', for Kenner, is that they 'draw the attention away from what the poet actually wrote on the page'.

> Macbeth in his despairing mood chooses to reduce life to a walking shadow, and it seems impertinent to say that he really meant only to compare the two. Similarly, to say that when he wrote 'How sweet the moonlight sleeps upon this bank!' Shakespeare was employing 'figurative language' equivalent to 'the moon is shining and I like it', is to distract us from noticing that he means us to feel the moonlight as something literally sleeping, and the spectacle of that sleep as something sweet.[18]

Kenner, in talking about 'an image', is still thinking of it as something to do with metaphor; but he has a special modern theory of metaphors, according to which they are not really comparisons at all. If a poet compares A to B, he *means* B, and means you to realise B so thoroughly that you might almost as well forget about A (as a Symbolist poet presents you with the 'objective correlative' of his meaning without naming the meaning itself at all).

And if you were going to talk about 'images', there would be a lot in favour of talking about them in Kenner's way. Since, for one thing, it steers clear of the whole confusing and irrelevant subject of mental imagery. Confucius's dish works in the way it does in the sentence quoted because of what we know about dishes:

> we think of the dish as an implement, something *used* (the 'proper man' isn't used by anybody); as an object into which you put things (the proper man doesn't passively submit to being 'filled up'), as distinguished from, say, a spring or a well; but an object into which you can't put very much, as distinguished from a pot or a barrel . . .[19]

and not because we visualise it in any particular way. And further, by implying that responding properly to 'images' is much the same as responding properly to language (live, not dead language) in general, Kenner avoids the awkward suggestion that 'images' are a special sort of non-linguistic device, called in to help language out.

None the less, it is fairly easy to demolish Kenner's theory. For, though what he says about the way words define each other by juxtaposition is very well said, it doesn't only apply when there are 'things' named in the sentence. The same precision and richness can be got by juxtaposing abstract words, as in Shakespeare's 'Ripeness is all', or Dante's 'E'n la sua voluntade è nostra pace'.

Then again, Kenner says that it is the presence of *things* (combined with rhythm) in a sentence which 'locks the meaning down to the page'. It is this which can make writing imperishable (so that, whereas we have laboriously to reconstruct the meaning of Wordsworth's 1800 Preface and its key-words 'nature', 'imagination' and 'soul', his poem 'She dwelt among the untrodden ways', since it names *things*—a violet, a mossy stone—communicates as freshly as the day it was written). And it is this, again, according to Kenner, which makes it possible to translate without essential damage.—But the truth is, literature has all sorts of ways by which it 'locks its meaning down to the page', and achieves imperishability, despite change and decay in the meaning of words. The words 'staying' and 'waftage', so crucial to the effect of Shakespeare's

> I stalk about her door,
> Like a strange soul upon the Stygian banks
> Staying for waftage.

have shifted in meaning since Shakespeare wrote them, yet these marvellous lines make their effect unerringly. And try translating *them* into another language 'without essential damage'!

Kenner's account of 'images' is crippled by a crude doctrine about 'things' and their place in literature. Using 'images', for Kenner, is a matter of getting *things* into your writing, and he remarks that 'Any image is by its nature more vivid than any statement.' Well, of course, as a moment's reflection will tell you, it isn't true—at least if 'vividness' has anything to do with vigour, forcibility or liveliness. Yeats's 'The best lack all conviction, while the worst Are full of passionate intensity' is incomparably forceful, in its context, though it names no 'things'. There is something narrow and doctrinaire about this insistence on *things* in poetry. It is admirable, and yet faintly comic when Kenner argues that

> to say that when he wrote 'How sweet the moonlight sleeps

upon this bank!' Shakespeare was employing 'figurative language', equivalent to 'the moon is shining and I like it', is to distract us from noticing that he means us to feel the moonlight as something literally sleeping, and the spectacle of that sleep as something sweet.[20]

Not *literally*, surely? Not *literally* literally? The word spoils the argument by over-statement. And though he is ready to admit, with a shade of irony, that terms like 'metaphor' and 'simile' and 'synecdoche' have 'many uses', it is plain that he personally hasn't much use for them, and that he thinks the distinction between a metaphor and a simile trivial. Such terminology 'draws the attention away from what the poet actually wrote on the page'. The fact that Wordsworth writes 'A violet by a mossy stone' but 'Fair *as* a star' hardly signifies for him, compared with the fact that the violet and the star are both palpably 'there'—things presented for their own sake. And here Kenner is failing to attend to 'what the poet actually wrote on the page'. For 'as' is one of the words on the page, and to ignore the word 'as' on principle is to ignore a whole range of expressive possibilities. In this poem it is exactly the 'as' which gives the subtlety and equivocal flavour to what Wordsworth is saying. Is he being eulogistic (Lucy was *particularly* fair) or grudging (she looked fair, as there were no rivals to put her in the shade)?

If critical theory can do anything to help a writer, it is perhaps to enlarge his sense of the infinite variety of expressive resources. And any principle which tends to blunt this sense—or even, like Kenner's, to sharpen it in one direction whilst blunting it in another—must be a bad one.

* * *

There is a very fine essay by F. R. Leavis, 'Imagery and movement: Notes in the analysis of poetry', which is, in many ways, an ideal corrective to these problems and confusions. The essay contains some superb model analyses of passages from Donne, Keats, Wordsworth and others, and its whole burden is that, when a critic uses terms like 'imagery' and 'movement', it doesn't matter if he can't define them precisely. They are to be used in a tentative and purely pragmatic way, and if they lead to sensitive perception, they have done their job.

> The point has been sufficiently made that in considering these kinds of effect we find 'imagery' giving place to 'movement' as the appropriate term for calling attention to what has to be analysed. That we cannot readily define just where 'imagery' ceases to be an appropriate term need cause no inconvenience, and there seems no more profit in attempting a definition of 'movement' than of 'imagery'. The important thing is to be as aware as possible of the ways in which life in verse may manifest itself—life, or that vital organisation that makes collections of words poetry. Terms must be made means to the necessary precision by careful use in relation to the concrete; their use is justified in so far as it is shown to favour sensitive perception; and the precision in analysis aimed at is not to be attained by seeking formal definitions as its tools. It is as pointers for use—*in* use—in the direct discussion of pieces of poetry that our terms and definitions have to be judged . . . [21]

All I have said against Clemen and Rugoff, etc., has been said better by Leavis in this essay. He is emphatic that 'images' and the like are not things you can isolate and draw a circle round:

> it will not do to treat metaphors, images and other local effects as if their relation to the poem were at all like that of plums to cake. They are worth examining—they are there to examine—because they are foci of a complex life, and sometimes the context from which they cannot be even provisionally separated, if the examination is to be worth anything, is a wide one.[22]

The 'essential heads in analysing the effects of interesting metaphor or imagery', he says, are *tone* and 'attitude towards'. And if he is right, then it clearly can't do much good to start counting and mapping 'images'. They can't be docketed in terms of their content, and it means nothing that there should be 145 or 227 'disease-images' in *Hamlet*—a strange piece of information about a work of literature, useful only to an observer from another planet. Talking of 'images' at all is only very provisional for Leavis: certain phenomena 'invite the description *image*', but it would do almost as well to think of them as 'movement'—and no-one has thought of counting up how many times an author uses the same kind of 'movement'. And if 'tone' and 'attitude towards' are embodied in 'images' or 'movement', they are also embodied in many other things simultaneously—for instance, the quality of a particular rhyme, or the contrast between one scene of a play and the next.

Moreover, if the words 'image' and 'movement', for Leavis, are not to be rigidly defined, and 'must be made means to the necessary precision by careful uses in relation to the concrete', the same is even more true of the word 'concrete'. It has been argued by J. Kilham, in an article in the *British Journal of Aesthetics*,* that the word 'concreteness' turns up in so many different senses in *The Great Tradition* that it really stands for very little—nothing much more than general approval. I think he more or less proves his point—but not in a way very damaging to Leavis. What Leavis's use of the word comes down to is something definite, but very general: a demand of the *writer* that he should have a sure grasp of the actual; and a demand of a *work* that it should exhibit a full and conscientious 'doing' (the same demand as Henry James is making when he complains of Meredith's *Lord Ormont and his Aminta* 'Not a difficulty met, not a figure presented, not a scene constituted').

In demanding that a writer should have a sure grasp of the actual, Leavis is in line with a broad stream of Romantic and post-Romantic criticism. Respect for the fact, patient scrutiny of natural forms, belief (like that of Hopkins) that revelation comes from scrupulous attentiveness to 'things' in all their uniqueness and selfhood—that campaign, begun by Blake, against the generalising habits of Augustanism with Sir Joshua Reynolds as the arch-enemy; all these are present behind Leavis's central doctrine, as a distant chorus of voices. But his insight into the medium of verse and his understanding of what it is and what it is not (his own superior 'grasp of the actual' as a critic, indeed) enables him to hold the doctrine in the most right and helpful way for a critic. Among the major English critics, Leavis is peculiar in placing so much emphasis on how verse is actually experienced. He always stresses the fact that poetry consists of words to be repeated in certain prescribed and invariable order. Poetry is not scanned or contemplated, like

---

* 'The use of "Concreteness" as an evaluative term in F. R. Leavis's *The Great Tradition*' (*British Journal of Aesthetics*, vol. 5, no. 1 (1965).

painting and sculpture. It can only come into being by dint of a reader performing, silently or out loud, a set succession of vocal gestures. And by following this drill, by 'realising' the meaning of the words under the strict control and guidance of rhythm and the shape of the verse-lines, the reader puts himself in the poet's shoes and has the illusion, as Leavis says, of 'living that particular action, situation or piece of life'.

Leavis is much more definite than the other major English critics in regarding poetry as a mimetic art, and he is constantly pointing out how a particular formal effect 'enacts' the meaning —for instance in his well-known comments on Donne's 'On a huge hill. . . . ' etc. from *Satire III.*

> This is the Shakespearian use of English, one might say that it is the English use—the use, in the essential spirit of the language, of its characteristic resources. The words seem to do what they say; a very obvious example of what, in more or less subtle forms, is pervasive being given in the image of reaching that the reader has to enact when he passes from the second to the third line.[23]

It follows from this that in speaking of 'concreteness', or in holding that a poet requires a secure grasp of the actual, Leavis is not thinking of poetry as rendering 'things', but rather as rendering a man attending to things—as miming an attitude of scrupulous attentiveness.

There is an advantage in this, for criticism. For, as we have seen, literature, being, by the nature of its medium, irredeemably general, has an uneasy relationship with *things*—uneasy, I mean, as compared with painting and sculpture. Painting and sculpture, compelled by the nature of their medium to deal in the particular (a particular shape, a particular patch of colour), are on easy terms with *things*, and the problem and struggle for them is to attain to the general. Literature, on the other hand, being general, struggles and yearns towards the particular; but the nearest it can get to it is to mime the action of attending to the particular. (And how often poets, wanting to capture some unique quality in a thing, against the nature of language, are forced back on *saying* how unique it is:

> All this long eve so balmy and serene,
> Have I been gazing on the western sky,
> And its peculiar tint of yellow green . . .)

Nor is this such a limitation to literature as it sounds. For there is always something a little mystical in the belief that 'things' in themselves contain truth or revelation. It can be a strong support and inspiration; but it is none the less an illusion: the truth and revelation come not from the things themselves but from the habit and discipline of attentiveness to them. And a grasp of the actual does not necessarily have anything to do with objects. It is not more evident in poets with a devotion to objects, like Hopkins, than in, say, Valéry, who found it impossible to take objects seriously. The actual which Valéry grasped, and which his verse shows him in the act of faithfully attending to, was of another kind.

The notion of 'concreteness' tends to be twinned with the discussion of 'imagery'—sometimes in a simple-minded way, as if 'images' were somehow a quite different sort of thing from words and brought a solid lump of reality intact onto the page. So it is interesting to notice a most suggestive and enlightening remark in Leavis's essay:

> Whenever in poetry we come on places of especially striking 'concreteness'—places where the verse has such life and body that we hardly seem to be reading arrangements of words—we may expect analysis to yield notable instances of the copresence in complex effects of the disparate, the conflicting or the contrasting.[24]

These occasions when 'the verse has such life and body that we hardly seem to be reading arrangements of words' have a special importance for him. He talks rather in the same manner about Comus's great speech. 'The total effect is as if words as words withdrew themselves from the focus of our attention and we were directly aware of a tissue of feelings and perceptions.' And there are clearly cases where words are being used with the highest possible complexity: words 'withdraw themselves from the focus of our attention' through the very intensity of their organisation, as a spinning top seems to stand still. But what is significant here is that 'concreteness'—at least in this context—springs from the effort to reconcile conflicting and contrasting ideas. Concreteness is bound up with that most strenuously ratiocinative thing, metaphor, and with the fact about metaphor with which this book began—that it involves two conflicting things, only held together by imaginative effort, and ready to spring apart again at any moment.

> It is from some such complexity as this, involving the telescoping or focal coincidence in the mind of contrasting or discrepant impressions or effects that metaphor in general —live metaphor—seems to derive its life; life involves friction and tension—a sense of arrest—in some degree.[25]

The efficacy and expressiveness of a metaphor depends on the effort and activity involved—the particular length and particular kind of effort and casting-around which is imposed on the reader in his attempt to 'realise' it. And to use the term 'image', which suggests something inert and single, like a painting or an idol or a reflection in a mirror, to describe this activity seems bound to lead to confusion. It is only because Leavis is so careful to pay no more than lip-service to any piece of terminology—because he is writing in a style so unlike the traditional language of exposition and argument—that he can use the word with impunity.

4

'CONCRETENESS'

I have said that the subject of 'concreteness' tends to be twinned in people's minds with that of 'imagery', and I had better pursue this now; for it has a bearing on our whole subject.

The one weakness in Ray Frazer's article 'The origin of the word "image"' (p. 27) is the jump it makes from Renaissance metaphors to the Imagist movement—overleaping so many historic revolutions. Here is the passage:

> In the Renaissance, descriptions of natural objects were almost always the minor terms of figures, illustrations or examples . . . Herrick's little lyric is not about daffodils but about a memento mori. The Renaissance poet is usually explicit. The relationship he sees between the image and the idea is logically explained. Since his time there has been a gradual shift away from logic and away from explanation: a twentieth-century Imagist poem contains only the image. 'Pre-Romantic' nature poetry of the eighteenth century is a step in the modern direction. Though still explicit, even garrulous, the nature poet is not merely using imagery for some logical purpose, but celebrating it—or celebrating his own sensitive response to it.[1]

And certainly it's true that Renaissance poets were not interested in describing real daffodils, but only emblematic ones; but then that says something about, not how they felt about daffodils, but how they felt about description. Their descriptions of the human figure were equally emblematic—that is to say they were concerned with what the writer 'knew' to be there in the subject, rather than what he merely observed.

And at the same time, the writers of Herrick's period could, as we know, be intensely 'concrete'. In Eliot's phrase, they enjoyed 'direct sensuous apprehension of thought', they had the 'intellect . . . immediately at the tips of the senses'. This is felt to be one of their great strengths—the quality, say, of Jonson's lines in *Volpone*:

> You shall have some will swallow
> A melting heir as glibly as your Dutch
> Will pills of butter, and ne'er purge for it;
> Tear forth the fathers of poor families
> Out of their beds, and coffin them alive
> In some kind clasping prison, where their bones
> May be forthcoming, when the flesh is rotten:

—and it began to disappear from English poetry at the Restoration. 'Concreteness', at least in seventeenth-century poetry, was a concomitant of wit; and, by banishing the conceit, the writers of the Restoration were also banishing 'concreteness'. It was a quality noticeably absent from the new landscape poets, of whom it would be fair to say, not only what Eliot said of eighteenth- and nineteenth-century poets in general, that 'they thought and felt by fits, unbalanced; they reflected', but that that was their intention.

'Concreteness', that is to say, turns out to have nothing intrinsically to do with recording observation—whether scientific observation, which was what Sprat was thinking about in calling for 'primitive purity, and shortness' in prose: or poetic observation of landscape, as found in the verse of Thomson and Young. Its presence or absence in English verse has nothing much to do with the rise of 'Nature-poetry' or the 'celebration of natural images for their own sake'. Keats was an intensely 'concrete poet', whilst Wordsworth was a relatively un-concrete one, yet their devotion to Nature was much of the same kind.

As for the *demand* for 'concreteness' or 'sensuous immediacy' from poetry, as an explicit doctrine, on the part of poets and critics, this really needs to be seen in the context of that fairly recent movement—much later in date than either the Augustans or the Romantics—which placed truth and significance in *things* alone: 'No ideas but in things', in William Carlos Williams's famous phrase.

To ask how this movement came into being is to ask the most general question possible about modern literature. It is, in the broadest way, bound up with the decline of religious belief. Joseph Hillis Miller, in *The Disappearance of God* and

Poets of Reality, has described the whole development of modern English literature—I think rather convincingly—in terms of two stages in writers' attitude to God. For nineteenth-century writers such as De Quincey, Browning, Emily Brontë, Matthew Arnold, and Hopkins, he says, God had disappeared from the universe—he had mysteriously gone out of reach; he was a *deus absconditus*, removed to some hiding-place where by no effort could he be found. For twentieth-century writers, in the other hand, such as Yeats, Eliot, Dylan Thomas, Wallace Stevens and William Carlos Williams, God, or eternity, exist—if they exist anywhere—in the here and now: in the instant, and the concrete, and in 'things'—things glimpsed in the moment before the mind has had time to generalise and categorise them.

> He that sings a lasting song
> Thinks in the marrow-bone.

Twentieth-century writers, to survive, feel they must 'step barefoot into reality'.

It might be tempting to regard this development as the completion of a cultural cycle. God, in the most primitive stages of thought, was located in stocks and stones; then (at the stage of the great religions) in Heaven; then (with the Romantic movement) in the human breast; and finally, in the most recent era, once again in stocks and stones. And certainly, I need hardly say, primitivism has played a large part in twentieth-century intellectual movements. But it would be a cheap paradox, all the same. For, as it turns out, 'primitivism' is not a very helpful angle from which to view this desire of twentieth-century writers for 'unmediated vision'.* At least, (and this is a serious objection), it seems hard to use the term 'primitivism' except in a slightly derogatory way. And, what is more to the point, no reader of Lévi-Strauss's *The Savage Mind* will believe that this 'primitivism' has much to do with the primitive. The most characteristic things about the 'savage

* See Geoffrey Hartman, *The Unmediated Vision*, Yale, 1954. Hartman argues that, for the modern poet, 'the *res creatae* are no longer known as an object of contemplation leading the observer by degrees to God, but as one compelling him to God through the intuition of an inconceivable physical force felt present equally in every particular thing' (p. 162).

mind', from Lévi-Strauss's account of it, seems to be that it is tirelessly and fanatically logical. It is never happy until, by totemic or other means, it has rationalised and classified the universe down to its minutest items, and by the most complex rules of inversion and transformation. Primitive man turns out to be quite as Linnaean as he is Laurentian, and the fact that his logic is 'concrete' rather than abstract does not make it any less rational.

At all events, this twentieth-century viewpoint is, in the first place, not a doctrine about the nature of art and literature, but a theory, or a family of theories, about the nature of existence. However, much modernist aesthetic doctrine, from Symbolism onwards, has had the effect of pointing the way—given such a view of existence—that literature should go. For instance, the Imagist doctrine of 'not explaining'—the view that a poem should 'present', without discursive or explanatory scaffolding ('direct treatment of the object', etc.) fits in very well with the philosophical view that ideas are to be looked for, and looked for only, in 'things'. For if truth and ideas live in things—not in what you bring to things, but what you discover in them—then any *explanation* must be an obstacle to perceiving them; it will represent precisely those preconceptions which put a veil between the human mind and 'things'.

And the Imagist movement has left its mark even on poetry that has returned to 'explanation'. Poets of our own age are still fond of leaving the reader with a thing, or object, as the culmination of a train of thought—with the implication that it is the object which explains the thought, and not the thought the object. The object, by its dominating position, seems not merely to incarnate the sense of the poem but to transcend it—as if to say that no object can ever be finally exhausted by explanation.

There is something of this kind in a fine poem 'Out', by Ted Hughes, which I will have to quote at length, though I'm mainly concerned with the last line.

OUT

I

The Dream Time

My father sat in his chair recovering
From the four-year mastication by gunfire and mud,
Body buffeted wordless, estranged by long soaking
In the colours of mutilation. His outer perforations

Were valiantly healed, but he and the hearth-fire, its
blood-flicker
On biscuit-bowl and piano and table-leg,
Moved into strong and stronger possession
Of minute after minute, as the clock's tiny cog
Laboured and on the thread of his listening
Dragged him bodily from under
The mortised four-year strata of dead Englishmen
He belonged with. He felt his limbs clearing
With every slight, gingerish movement. While I, small
and four,
Lay on the carpet as his luckless double,
His memory's buried, immovable anchor,
Among jawbones and blown-off boots, tree-stumps, shell-
cases and craters,
Under rain that goes on drumming its rods and thickening
Its kingdom, which the sun has abandoned, and where nobody
Can ever again move from shelter.

II

The dead man in his cave beginning to sweat;
The melting bronze visor of flesh
Of the mother in the baby-furnace—
Nobody believes, it
Could be nothing, all
Undergo smiling at
The lulling of blood in
Their ears, their ears, their ears, their eyes
Are only drops of water and even the dead man suddenly
Sits up and sneezes—Atishoo!
Then the nurse wraps him up, smiling,
And, though faintly, the mother is smiling,
And it's just another baby.

As after being blasted to bits
The reassembled infantryman
Tentatively totters out, gazing around with the eyes
Of an exhausted clerk.

III

Remembrance Day

The poppy is a wound, the poppy is the mouth

Of the grave, maybe of the womb searching—

A canvas-beauty puppet on a wire
Today whoring everywhere. It is years since I wore one.

It is more years
The shrapnel that shattered my father's paybook

Gripped me, and all his dead
Gripped him to a time

He no more than they could outgrow, but, cast into one, like iron,
Hung deeper than refreshing of ploughs

In the woe-dark under my mother's eye—
One anchor

Holding my juvenile neck bowed to the dunkings of the Atlantic.
So goodbye to that bloody-minded flower.

You dead bury your dead.
Goodbye to the cenotaphs on my mother's breasts.

Goodbye to all the remaindered charms of my father's survival.
Let England close. Let the green sea-anemone close.

Paraphrasing the last line brutally: if the England of the 1914–18 war won't renounce its claims on the new generation, but still must try to drag it down into the Atlantic of deathly memories, then let England itself sink back into the Atlantic instead. Let it 'close', as a shop closes; but also as a sea-anemone closes—upon itself. The line draws together two separate strands of simile (just as, of course, it resolves a shifting conflict of attitudes). Memories of 1914–18 have been associated with blood—the blood of a birth in reverse, a birth backwards into the womb; and with water—the memories are a heavy anchor dragging the new generation down into the ocean of backwards-turned feeling. And these two strands are joined when the red or blood-coloured Remembrance Day flower is identified with the green flower of the sea. But the effectiveness of this last line lies in the largeness, combined with swiftness, of the gesture. Almost before you have had time to take in the complex comparison to the sea-anemone—the whole British

Isles, with their traditional green pastures, reduced to a mere marine plant (pretty and faintly sinister) on the beach of Europe—you have also to enact a wish about it, make it *do* something, have the sea-anemone close its petals. The poem is not startingly modern, but it clearly could not have been written by Wordsworth or Matthew Arnold. It has taken over something from Imagism in the device of letting the *thing* (the sea-anemone) come first before its explanation, or rather without any explicit explanation. This has the result, slightly, of tipping the balance of emphasis on to the 'thing' part of the comparison. Of course all the force and vividness of our apprehension of that sea-anemone comes from the intense activity of comparing that is going on, and the intense verse-shaping activity that goes hand in hand with this—the way we are catapulted into this comparison. But the ultimate effect is of being returned, in an un-Wordsworthian and un-Arnoldian way, to *things*, in their inexhaustibility.

Ted Hughes's poem puts me in mind also of a recent (very beautiful) poem by Philip Larkin.

HIGH WINDOWS

When I see a couple of kids
And guess he's fucking her and she's
Taking pills or wearing a diaphragm,
I know this is paradise

Everyone old has dreamed of all their lives—
Bonds and gestures pushed to one side
Like an outdated combine harvester,
And everyone young going down the long slide

To happiness, endlessly. I wonder if
Anyone looked at me, forty years back,
And thought, *That'll be the life,*
No God any more, or sweating in the dark

About hell and that, or having to hide
What you think of the priest. He
And his lot will all go down the long slide
Like free bloody birds. And immediately

Rather than words comes the thought of high windows:
The sun-comprehending glass,
And beyond it, the deep blue air, that shows
Nothing, and is nowhere, and is endless.

Paraphrasing crudely again: feeling a recurrent, familiar little pang of envy at the sight of young lovers—thinking how much simpler life has been made for their generation, with no religious anxieties, no sexual taboos—but recognising this next moment as a stock fantasy of the middle-aged, the poet is prompted to wonder, did anyone look at *me* when I was young, with the same pang? And the response to this question comes to him not in the form of words, but in the shape of 'the thought of high windows'. What the high windows represent is the effort to imagine the lovers' situation truly, not just in terms of stock-fantasy; and imagining it truly entails picturing not just the lovers' situation but that of all human beings. The writer, who for good or evil possesses vision (is himself like 'high windows'), 'comprehends' the sun and the sunnyness of sexual happiness, and sees, behind it and beyond it, the immense, unfathomable, featureless vista which life presents, a vista which *shows* nothing, or perhaps, terrifyingly, simply shows *nothing*.

The rendering of the distancing of a commonplace envy, the effortless modulation of tone from the rancid opening to the exalted close, and the effect of opening-out in the last lines, are wonderful, I think. But I bring the poem in here because of a curiousness in its form. When the response to the writer's casual question to himself came in the shape, not of words, but of 'the thought of high windows'. Larkin was presented with the makings of a poem in the Imagist manner. He had pictured the high windows before he understood what they meant, and he might have written the poem in the same way—in a 'non-explaining' style. As it turned out, being Larkin, he chose to write a different kind of poem, a sort of natural history of an unwritten Imagist poem. But in fact he doesn't explain the high windows, only carries on the thought as if he had done so; and the poem therefore has some of the effect, without the form, of an Imagist poem. The sense goes: 'What came into my head was . . . and I shan't spell out its meaning to you . . . and moreover it will never *completely* explain itself.'

* * *

But if the doctrine of attending to 'things', with its corollary of 'not explaining', had a strong influence on the form of modernist works of literature, then so did the doctrine of the 'here and now'. For if you believe that God and eternity exist, if anywhere, in the here and now, in the 'eternal moment', then you are likely to be drawn to the theory of the 'eternal recurrence' of history. Since if every moment can be thought of as coming round again, then the contents of a moment need not be regarded as utterly contingent and fleeting. By willing its passing you are willing its return.

Certainly, many of the major 'modernist' writers seem to have been drawn to this doctrine of 'eternal recurrence': Joyce, who borrowed a version of it from Vico; Eliot, who took it over from Buddhist and Hindu theology and merged it with the Christian doctrine of Purgatory; and Yeats, who raided every kind of neo-platonic and theosophical source for his system of cycles and gyres. And this attraction to the doctrine of the 'eternal return' of history seems to have affinities with the love of 'modernist' writers for serpent-like and spiral form: as in *Finnegans Wake*, where the opening sentence is the completion of the concluding one, or *Four Quartets*, with its double axis, 'In my beginning is my end' and 'In my end is my beginning' (or again such 'cyclical' works as *The Rainbow* and *Women in Love* and *A la recherche du temps perdu*).

There is something especially characteristic of 'modernist' writers in this love of circularity. It confirmed them in their artist's role as 'beyond good and evil'—for if everything repeats itself, the ethics of conduct have no finality. Again, at least with the novelists, it was part of an effort to rescue Realism from a dead-end: to 'de-materialise it', appealing from the iron law and 'closed cases' of nineteenth-century fiction to the sense of a perpetually renewed present. And, further, it was one result of the general 'modernist' desire to make their larger works into water-tight wholes, Noah's arks riding out deluge and chaos; it was an aspect of their determination to create synoptic works, deliberately packing in the multifarious whole of something—one man's entire memories, or the whole of Dublin—into a single vessel, or unfolding it from a single seed.

* * *

Thus an attachment to the instant and to 'things' ('no ideas but in things') can hardly, as philosophy, be separated from the 'disappearance of God', and as a theory of poetry, from Symbolist and post-Symbolist theory in general. And the demand for ‘concreteness’ and ‘sensuous immediacy’ in poetry—so important to Eliot and to Leavis—also needs to be thought of in this very wide context.

And if a poet aims to grasp and appropriate *things* in all their uniqueness and ‘thinginess’, then one way to do so would seem to be, and by many has been felt to be, through ‘concreteness’ of language. However, as it turns out, grappling with ‘things’ in poetry does not necessarily produce ‘concreteness’. And here we are brought back to something very characteristic of literature as a medium. Modern literature has wrestled heroically with the ambition to bring words close to things, but the result has not been what you might expect. Think, for instance, of the work of Wallace Stevens. It is all about the problem of relating imagination to reality; and Stevens's ambition is a kind of poetry which shall *be* reality, in which words *are* what they signify. ‘The word must be the thing it represents; otherwise it is a symbol. It is a question of identity,’ he says in *Opus Posthumous*.

> The poem is the cry of its occasion
> Part of the res itself and not about it.

And his poems, in their elusive syntax and rhythm, render subtly—‘concretely’, if you like—the motions of a mind grappling with this problem. Still, it is not objects, but a problem about objects, or a man wrestling with this problem, which Stevens's poems are rendering.

> . . . And so the freed man said.
> It was how the sun came shining into his room:
> To be without a description of to be,
> For a moment on rising, at the edge of the bed, to be,
> To have the ant of the self changed to an ox
> With its organic boomings, to be changed
> From a doctor into an ox, before standing up,
> To know that the change and that the ox-like struggle
> Come from the strength that is the strength of the sun,
> Whether it comes directly or from the sun.
> It was how he was free. It was how his freedom came.
> It was being without description, being an ox,
> It was the importance of the trees outdoors,
> The freshness of the oak-leaves, not so much

That they were oak-leaves, as the way they looked.
It was everything being more real, himself
At the centre of reality, seeing it.
It was everything bulging and blazing and big in itself.
The blue of the rug, the portrait of Vidal,
Qui fait fi des joliesses banales, the chairs.*

It is not a language weighty with the pressure of things. And indeed Stevens's attitude to objects is a mixture of reverence and the most imperious and insouciant high-handedness; so that when he says that 'The word must be the thing it represents', we are not to think of 'thing' as meaning 'object' but something more like 'poem'.

But then, if we go back to Gerard Manley Hopkins, as a writer in whom a devotion to 'things', in their quiddity and 'sensuous particularity', does unquestionably go with an intensely 'concrete' style, what the 'concreteness', the packed density and muscularity of his style, seems to represent is the miming not so much of objects themselves as of the imaginative effort to grasp and seize them—not the objects, but the poet's wrestling with them. Indeed, mimicry, which is literature's one link with actuality more intimate than the mere relation of sign to thing signified (of the word 'tree' to the thing 'tree') tends to become trivial when applied to things, as opposed to human activities. Hence the obviousness and crudity of the effects labelled 'onomatopoeia' in the textbooks, and hence also the tendency of some critics (for instance, Yvor Winters) to deny that verse is a mimetic art at all.

Of course, critics who call for 'concreteness' from verse, and want words brought as close as possible to 'things', may not be thinking of 'sensuous particularity'. For instance, Fenollosa, in holding up Chinese ideographic writing as a model of how language should be brought close to 'things',[2] is not really concerned with the 'sensuous' qualities of experience or language. (Though indeed the gulf between ideographic and phonetic writing is so great, it is hardly possible to think of English learning from Chinese in this respect. You could hardly expect to find the counterpart of Hopkins in Chinese verse.) Fenollosa is thinking of another and more basic kind of mimesis, the one by which language itself—all language, at least in

* From 'The Latest Freed Man'.

origin—reproduces 'the universal form of action in nature'. According to Fenollosa the sentence-form itself was forced on man by nature. The basis of all speech consists in 'vivid shorthand pictures of action and processes in nature', and a language for intellectual operations is built up by using these in a metaphorical way. Metaphor is 'at once the substance of nature and of language'; and the work of poets, whose main instrument is metaphor, 'lies in feeling back along the ancient lines of advance'.

And though Fenollosa wants the words of poetry to stay as close as possible to 'things'—'the one necessity, even in our own poetry, is to keep words as flexible as possible, as full of the sap of nature'—by 'things' and 'nature' he doesn't mean objects but the forces working through objects. This is why he holds that 'The verb must be the primary fact of nature.'

> Relations are more real and more important than the things which they relate. The forces which produce the branch-angles of an oak lay potent in the acorn. Similar lines of resistance, half-curbing the out-pressing vitalities, govern the branching of rivers and of nations. Thus a nerve, a wire, a roadway, and a clearing-house are only varying channels which communication forces for itself.[3]

For Fenollosa the link between language and 'things' is a morphological one, and 'sensuousness' as a quality in poetic language is not one of his concerns.

On the other hand, it is one of the concerns of T. E. Hulme, another advocate of bringing words as close as possible to 'things'; at least this seems to be what's implied by his remark that 'Poetry . . . is not a counter language, but a visual concrete one. It is a compromise for a language of intuition which would hand over sensation bodily.'[4] However, that word 'compromise' points to a weak element in Hulme's poetics in general, not unlike one we found in Rémy de Gourmont's. It amounts to a vote of no-confidence in words, like the one passed by the professors in Swift's Lagado:

> We next went to the school of languages, where three professors sat in consultation upon improving that of their own country.
>
> The first project was, to shorten discourse, by cutting polysyllables into one, and leaving out verbs and

participles; because in reality all things imaginable are but nouns.

The other project was, a scheme for entirely abolishing all words whatsoever; and this was urged as a great advantage in point of health, as well as brevity. For it is plain, that every word we speak is, in some degree, a diminution of our lungs by corrosion; and consequently contributes to the shortening of our lives. An expedient was therefore offered, 'that since words are only names for things, it would be more convenient for all men to carry about them such things as were necessary to express a particular business they are to discourse on'. . . . many of the most learned and wise adhere to the new scheme of expressing themselves by things; which has only this inconvenience attending it, that if a man's business be very great, and of various kinds, he must be obliged, in proportion, to carry a greater bundle of things upon his back, unless he can afford one or two strong servants to attend him. I have often beheld two of these sages almost sinking under the weight of their packs, like pedlars among us; who, when they met in the street, would lay down their loads, open their packs, and hold conversation for an hour together; then put up their implements, help each other to resume their burdens, and take their leave.[5]

Donald Davie, in *Articulate Energy*, has done a great deal to clear our minds about the demand for 'concreteness' in verse. And I think one has to agree with him that to want to bring words as close as possible to 'things' is, strictly, an example of the very 'abstraction' which critics like Hulme and Fenollosa and Hugh Kenner attack. For what is 'concrete' in existence is experiences, not things; things are only an abstraction from experiences.

It follows that ideographic writing, in which words embody things, is *more abstract than* writing in which words are fiduciary symbols for elements of an experience.[6]

Concepts, and the apparatus of reasoning, are an inextricable part of reality, just as much as 'things'; they are not, as these critics would have it, a tiresome obstacle or veil put between us and reality by monkish logicians. And hence, as Davie argues, there is no reason to feel (as Hulme and others do) that syntax, which is the counterpart in language of this conceptual equipment, has no place in poetry.

A further point to be made, though, is that when critics speak of 'concreteness', there are two quite different things they may have in mind. They may mean the quality in words of being 'full of the sap of nature' (Fenollosa); or the capacity of verse or prose to embody the sensuous quality, the presence and life of things, so vividly that the words, as words, become transparent and disappear from our consciousness (Leavis); or the richness and precision of *meaning* attained by a language drawn from 'things' (Hugh Kenner). All these have a natural connection with one another. But on the other hand, they may mean the practice of 'not explaining'—the using of an 'objective correlative' to stand for an unstated, and otherwise incommunicable, subjective experience. There is a great gap between the two meanings, so much so that at first sight it's not too easy to see the connection. Mallarmé, and the Symbolists generally, were 'concrete' in the second sense, as a matter of poetic principle, but rarely in the first. One could hardly look for a flatter rejection of 'sensuous particularity' (or 'concreteness' in the first sense) than Mallarmé's

> A quoi bon la merveille de transposer un fait de nature en sa presque disparition vibratoire selon le jeu de la parole, cependant, si ce n'est pour qu'en émane, sans la gêne d'un proche ou concret rappel, la notion pure?[7]

(I rather despair of translating this, but perhaps one could roughly render:

> What, however, is the point of the miracle of transposing a fact of nature into a faint, almost-unheard, vibration, following the hazards of language, if not that it may distil, without the nuisance of a close or concrete evocation, the pure idea which it encloses?)

And I think one of the reasons why discussions of 'concreteness' often end up in paradox is that two very different trains of thought have converged and made use of the same term. Eliot's influence may have been important here, for both aspects of literature were very important to him and were intertwined in his theory of poetry, though the term 'concrete' itself was not one of his favourite ones.

This is a good moment to mention a brilliant contribution to the discussion of 'concreteness' by W. K. Wimsatt, in *The Verbal Icon.* Wimsatt begins by observing that the modern schoolbook maxim that writing, and especially description, ought to be as 'particular' or 'concrete' as possible is very hard to make sense of; and, in so far as it can, it seems rather a stifling prejudice. 'What is the right word for anything, the right degree of specification?' he asks. The answer is that it is a matter of the *decorum* of the particular work in hand. Since the plot of *The Spoils of Poynton* turns on objects (i.e. *objets d'art*), it was a fine stroke of Henry James's to make his opening description of Poynton almost completely abstract and unspecific. 'Since the same things may have to be mentioned many times in the course of one story, he is doubtless a wary craftsman who makes the first description a promise or a threat.'

However, so Wimsatt's argument goes, the trouble is, whereas it is easy enough to understand the word 'abstract' in an absolute sense (as when we say that the words 'truth' or 'justice' are abstractions), it is much harder to tell what is meant when the word is used to mean 'very general', or 'not very specific'. The only way to give this any precise meaning is by referring the word 'specific' to its congener 'species' and the concept of 'specific substance'. There is a sense in which we all feel that 'Man' is a better answer to the question 'What is it?' than 'vertebrate' or 'white man', and 'spade' a better answer than 'implement' or 'rusty garden spade'. 'Man' and 'spade' belong to what Wimsatt calls 'a kind of critical or vaporising line in the scale of generality. And discussions of 'abstractness' and 'concreteness' in writing take on more point if we divide writing by a table of styles, according to its position in regard to this line:

1. The abstract or less than specific-substantive style: e.g. *implement.*
2. The minimum concrete or specific-substantive style, e.g. *spade.*
3. The extra-concrete, the detailed, or more than specific style; e.g. *rusty garden spade.*

Jane Austen would, characteristically, come in the first category, and the Imagists in the third. And Wimsatt goes on to argue that fashions in preferring one or other of these levels are related to changing ideas about *species*: so that, when philosophers of the school of Locke and Hume began to undermine the dignity of proper names and essences, the reaction of poets was to resort to periphrases, to use phrases like 'scaly breed' or 'fleecy kind', which combine the first level with the third, leaving out the second level, the name, altogether.

No value-judgement is implied by Wimsatt's table: the point he is making is merely that if the terms 'concrete', 'specific' and 'particular' are going to be used in value-judgements about literature they need to be referred to this concept of 'specific substance'. He goes on to argue, however, that the idea of 'specific substance' has a particular significance for *metaphor*: since for something to be a metaphor at all, rather than a mere analogy, there has to be specific difference as well as similarity. (It's a metaphor when you call a man a skunk, but merely an analogy if you say of a traitor than he is 'another Judas'.*) Hence he is inclined to regard the sort of metaphor used by the metaphysical poets, in which both vehicle and tenor are specifically named objects, as the most natural and fundamental kind, 'a sort of special fulfilment of the essential direction of metaphor towards concrete rather than abstract predication'.

I have given only the roughest sketch of Wimsatt's subtle essay. But one thing it brings home forcibly is that even the three interpretations of 'concreteness' I have grouped together—the Fenollosa, Leavis and Kenner ones—are a pretty loose assemblage. Wimsatt's example of a style sticking strictly to his second, or 'specific substantive', level is taken from Swift. And he reminds us that Swift, for all his irony against the professors of Lagado, is a master of the art of persuading the reader he is encountering not words but things: he achieves it by a style of absolute plainness—one which could hardly have less 'sensuous immediacy', and merely names things. Thus:

> The kingdom is a peninsula, terminated to the northeast by a ridge of mountains thirty miles high, which are altogether impassable by reason of the volcanoes upon the tops. Neither do the most learned know what sort of mortals inhabit beyond these mountains, or whether they be inhabited at all. On the other three sides it is bounded by ocean. There is not a sea-port in the whole kingdom.

* See my own remarks on page 71.

Wimsatt's essay also reminds us that we tend, lazily, to talk as if 'general' meant much the same as 'abstract', and 'particular' much the same as 'concrete'. Whereas, for example, the passage from Swift I have just quoted is very general, but the very opposite of abstract (it 'calls a spade a spade'). Whilst on the other hand Henry James, though he is always abstracting, almost never generalises. At whatever level of abstraction he is writing, it is always the specific case which interests him.

And one last remark, of a different kind, prompted by this essay. If Locke and Hume forced poets to give up naming and specifying things, Darwin, in similar circumstances, had almost the opposite effect. It was Darwin's unsettling of 'species'—or at least this was one of the main factors—which inspired Gerard Manley Hopkins to his impassioned defence of the quiddity and *haeccitas* of 'things'.

* * *

I have said that the demand for 'concreteness' has to be understood in the context of the literary movement which places truth and significance in 'things'. But perhaps it is wrong to speak of this as a movement at all, for it seems to take in so much. So many major figures would, in their own way, have to have a place in it: Pound, Wallace Stevens, William Carlos Williams, Rilke in his *Neue Gedichte* period, let alone the many minor figures who have based their whole poetics upon attention to 'things'—poets like Elizabeth Bishop, Francis Ponge, Geoffrey Grigson or Charles Tomlinson. One would really be talking about a major part of twentieth-century verse. (And the novelists of the *nouveau roman* would have to be thought of in close relationship to such a movement; though Robbe-Grillet, at least, is not interested in 'things' as such, only in tracing the frontier between things and humanity.)

However, Hugh Kenner has made a strong case for some such 'movement' or reorientation as having been a real event in literary history; and he thinks of it as having its beginnings well before the twentieth century, and with a novelist. He regards Flaubert's discovery that everything can be said through the juxtaposition of things or 'assembled particulars' as being 'the major intellectual *peripeteia* of the past eighty years' (he is writing in 1951), and says that 'Literary histories will henceforth be meaningless until they can take account of this change'.

I think myself that it does make some sense to speak of it as a movement. And I believe, too, that it helps to consider the demand for 'concreteness' in verse in the context of it. All the same, with William Carlos Williams, who gave this movement its most famous formulation—'Say it! No ideas but in things.'—the concept of 'concreteness' is already beginning to lose its meaning.

Williams's poems are 'concrete' in both the senses we have been discussing—some in one sense, and some in the other. He produces poems on the principle of 'not explaining'—I mean, of giving no indication why we should attach significance to the facts he is mentioning. For instance in

POEM

As the cat
climbed over
the top of

the jamcloset
first the right
forefoot

carefully
then the hind
stepped down

into the pit of
the empty
flowerpot

And here the writing is purely denotatory (as general in its expression as it is particular in its content). It makes no attempt at all to draw on the potential richness, the 'tentacular roots', of language. All the strength lies in the movement of the verse, which reflects the movement of a mind apprehending one thing after another—progressing by atomic steps, as if in between each step the world had been annihilated and recreated. Though the poem is 'concrete' in the sense of 'not explaining', nothing could be less 'concrete' in the other sense than this language, which merely names things. Each new word or phrase is meant to dawn on the page with Edenic purity, as if one were meeting it for the first time and there were no need to use poetic arts to bring out its richness.

Elsewhere, on the other hand, his language has density and is pregnant with the sensuous presence of things; it is language which offers resistance when (in his own words) 'the world comes towards him to brush against the spines of his shrub'. For instance, in these rich lines from 'The Lonely Street':

> . . . They have grown tall. They hold
> pink flames in their right hands.
> In white from head to foot,
> with sidelong, idle look—
> in yellow, floating stuff,
> black sash and stockings—
> touching their avid mouths
> with pink sugar on a stick— . . .

or in his lovely and rather Poundian still-life 'The Pot of Flowers':

> Pink confused with white
> flowers and flowers reversed
> take and spill the shaded flame
> darting it back
> into the lamp's horn
>
> petals aslant darkened with mauve
>
> red where in whorls
> petal lays its glow upon petal
> round flamegreen throats
>
> petals radiant with transpiercing light
> contending
> above
> the leaves
> reaching up their modest green
> from the pot's rim
>
> and there, wholly dark, the pot
> gay with rough moss.

But the notion of 'concreteness' doesn't, after all, seem very relevant to Williams; for, to be 'concrete', a writer depends on a framework of traditional expectations. The reader has to be responding to the feat by which the poet charges a conventional metrical arrangement of words in such a way that 'things' appear to break through, making him forget he is reading words at all. If the frame of expectations is removed, there is no longer any feat of this kind to respond to. And Williams's poems, from one point of view, are essentially 'frameless'. His poems, characteristically, don't arrive at any conclusion; at any point in their progress the slate may be wiped clean and a fresh start made. This is inherent in their nature; for if they achieve their purpose of apprehending the 'here and now' of the world, then there is nothing for them to do but to begin the same attempt over again.

Of course, this is only half the story with Williams. His poems also have a traditional aspect, as important to him as their 'frameless' one; and in his late period he arrived at a technical solution—the 'variable foot'—which gave metrical expression to the mixture of freedom and tradition that he wanted.

> We have today to do with the poetic, as always, but a *relatively* stable foot, not a rigid one. That is all the difference.
> It is that which must become the object of our search.
> Only by coming to that realisation should we escape the power of those magnificent verses of the past which we have always marveled over and still be able to enjoy them.[8]

But with a more recent writer in the Williams tradition, Gary Snyder, there is so little 'frame' or convention left that, though his poems are full of scrupulously observed items, it ceases to make any sense to use the word 'concrete' of them. There is plenty of close attention to 'things' in a poem like 'A Walk':

> Sunday the only day we don't work:
> Mules farting around the meadow,
>   Murphy fishing.
> The tent flaps in the warm
> Early sun: I've eaten breakfast and I'll
>   take a walk
> To Benson Lake. Packed a lunch.
> Goodbye. Hopping on creekbed boulders
> Up the rock throat three miles
>   Piute Creek—
> In steep gorge glacier-slick rattlesnake country
> Jump, land by a pool, trout skitter,
> The clear sky. Deer tracks.
> Bad place by a falls, boulders big as houses,
> Lunch tied to a belt,
> I stemmed up a crack and almost fell

But rolled out safe on a ledge
    and ambled on.
Quail chicks freeze underfoot, color of stone
Then run cheep! away, hen quail fussing.
Craggy west end of Benson Lake—after edging
Past dark creek pools on a long white slope—
Lookt down in the ice-black lake
    lined with cliff
From far above: deep shimmering trout.
A lone duck in a gunsightpass
    steep side hill
Through slide-aspen and talus, to the east end,
Down to grass, wading a wide smooth stream
Into camp. At last.
    By the rusty three-year-
Ago left-behind cookstove
Of the old trail crew.
Stoppt and swam and ate my lunch.

but there is hardly any desire to give the things a different value from what they would have in real life. Likewise, though the poem is full of Poundian rhythms, they create no pattern of expectations; and this is appropriate, because the fiction at work in the poem (and of course any good poetry requires a fiction) is that the writer is living a tract of experience in a wholly unpredictive, uncategorising, way. The relationship—between the content and some norm or 'frame', or between things inside the poem and the same things outside it—has largely gone, and with it any need to talk of 'concreteness'.

It is interesting to notice, though, that the demand for 'concreteness' and the wish to abolish the gap between the abstractness of language and the particularity and 'thinginess' of things are really rather close to the wish felt by many critics, from Gourmont onwards, that metaphors should 'come true'. According to this school of thought, either the thing compared and the thing it is compared to should have equal status and rights, in the way Richard Kostelanetz describes apropos of *Finnegans Wake*:

> What Joyce did . . . was to transcend the metaphoric relation—that one story is like another—for associations

that, as they eliminate the metaphoric dimension completely, transform analogies into identities.[9]

Or the original thing compared should be altogether suppressed, leaving only the thing it is compared to—which can then be regarded as if it were any other 'real' object. 'Pourquoi doubler l'image?' Pound, as we have seen, is always coming back to Henri Barzun's question. For writers in the Imagist and Vorticist traditions the element of comparison and duality in metaphor was an embarrassment and something to be overcome as far as possible. And here we come back to the word 'image'—since this is one of the reasons why they favoured the word. For whereas 'metaphor' suggests an activity—relating something to something, thinking of something in terms of something else—'image' suggests, though rather equivocally, a *thing*: something you could actually observe, like an idol or a photograph. And if 'images' are what a writer is producing, why should he have to produce them in pairs? *Pourquoi doubler l'image*? The word 'image', at a stroke, cut through the whole issue of duality raised by metaphor.

However, the trouble with the word 'image', and why Pound and T. E. Hulme found it so slippery to use, is that it is a term so remote from the *medium* of poetry. As I have said before, the basic material of poetry, words, is incurably general. Each word you use stands for a whole class of things, a genus or species; you say 'tree', and you have named all the trees in the world; you say 'John', and still you have named a whole forest of conflicting attributes. And whilst Donald Davie has reminded us that there is no reason to think of any part of language as more 'abstract' than any other, the sense in which poetry is a concrete, not an abstract, thing—the way in which it links up with real existence—is special to itself; it is nothing to do with 'images', which are the perquisite of painting and sculpture, it is a matter of mimicry. You can, if you like, speak of words having 'physical' properties as well as meaning; but these are not properties like thickness or smoothness or height, they are the properties of making a reader perform certain actions, or imagined actions, of the lips and tongue.

If all art is 'mimesis' or 'imitation', the different arts are imitative in different ways, and I think that it helps to think of literary mimesis as 'mimicry'—the word most commonly used of *verbal* imitations. The word tends to remind you of the characteristic thing about the literary medium, as opposed to painting and sculpture—the fact that it is an active medium, requiring the reader to go through a sort of performance. If it is to be more than a respectful bow to Aristotle to speak of art as 'imitation', one needs to keep a very firm sense of the medium of the art one is talking about. W. K. Wimsatt's term for literary imitation, 'iconicity',[10] seems to me awkward, just because it sets the mind running on the visual arts. There may be occasions when a parallel between poetry and painting is worth making, but obviously the very time not to make it is when you are talking about them as *media*—or there would be no sense in calling them 'poetry' and 'painting'. And from the point of view of the medium, whereas the basic material of painting (or at least figurative painting) is illusionism, the basic material of poetry is active mimicry.

The primary feature of verse as a medium, then, is its power to make the reader repeat precisely a particular sequence of actions, or imagined actions, of the lips and tongue and larynx—those and no other. (It is only under this strict control that its other elements can work—I mean, its power to make the reader re-enact imagined chains of feelings, and 'realise', or untie, knots of meaning). And here at once you have all the materials for mimicry. The reader, in taking in the lines, becomes like a stage-performer, 'taking-off' the (inward) gestures a man having certain experiences. And once you can place a reader in such a situation, you can then play off the plastic elements in verse against the meaning of the words to mimic all kinds of human behaviour (not 'things', but a man responding to things).

When we say that verse is 'expressive' we mean that something has been mimed successfully by it; and you can't really draw a sharp dividing line between 'expressiveness' in its most general sense and the crudely particular imitative devices called 'onomatopoeia' in textbooks of poetry.

They mount, they shine, evaporate, and fall*

---

* Unnumber'd suppliants crowd Preferment's gate,
Athirst for wealth, and burning to be great;
Delusive fortune hears the incessant call,
They mount, they shine, evaporate, and fall.
(Johnson, *The Vanity of Human Wishes*)

which so subtly enacts in its own curve the curve of the career of the 'unnumber'd suppliants' crowding 'Preferment's gate', is just as *mimetic* in its more complex and inward way as

> Dry clashed his harness in the icy caves

and the other old warhorses of 'onomatopoeia'. Notice for instance, how, with its lightness and swiftness, the four-syllable word 'evaporates' suggests the sudden dissipation of all that the previous four syllables, with their labour ('They mount, they shine') have achieved.

The uselessness of 'onomatopoeia' as a literary term is clear from its very definition; 'the sound echoing the sense'. For what is at work, always, if imitative devices are to have any value, is not the sound of the verse but the reader's activity in making the sounds, and the symbolic sensations and emotions accompanying this. And this takes us so far into the essential nature of poetry, the way in which poetry is 'expressive' at all, that one hardly needs to distinguish 'imitation' from 'expressiveness'. Consider the delicacy with which, in the last lines of Book 4 of *Paradise Lost*

> The Fiend lookt up and knew
> His mounted scale aloft: nor more; but fled
> Murmuring, and with him fled the shades of night.

the motion of a pair of scales is suggested, with 'nor more' as its fulcrum. It is a definite piece of mimicry, or what Leavis has called 'analogical enactment', but so much absorbed into the substance of the verse, in which so many other effects are taking place at the same time, that one hardly wants to highlight it. Or consider, again, the quite different sort of mimicry represented by the line

> Illimitable Ocean without bound

in which, by the mere symmetry and logic of the placing of 'illimitable' on one side of 'Ocean' and its exact synonym 'without bound' on the other, the idea of infinite ocean is given mimetic reinforcement. And Donald Davie has shown, in a brilliant passage in *Articulate Energy*, how poetic syntax itself, independently of versification or the 'plastic' elements in verse, can be mimetic. (He distinguishes five different kinds of poetic syntax—'subjective', 'dramatic', 'objective', 'syntax like music' and 'syntax like mathematics', of which the first four are all mimetic—and work, one might add, by dint of the syntax's drawing attention to itself in some way, either by repetition or by surprise.)

To use 'concreteness' usefully as a literary term, then, you need to remind yourself, in a fairly simple way, of what the literary medium consists in; and you also need to bear in mind the philosophical and religious reasons why 'concreteness' should become a value. At which point we can turn in our tracks. For if the demand for 'concreteness' in verse is mixed up with the philosophical doctrine 'no ideas but in things', then so is the popularity of the word 'image'. For there is a feeling that if a poet fills his lines with 'images' he is thereby filling them with 'things'. It is a strongly held conviction, and—I think—not always a very beneficial one. It actually does harm to some contemporary poets, though none of those I've mentioned. You get the impression that they are conscientiously stuffing their poems full of 'things' beyond all natural desire, and against the bent of their sensibility. And I think that what they would say they were doing, if you asked them, is that they were filling their poems with 'images'.

Certainly, some modern poets have set great store by the terms 'image' and 'imagery'. And this ought to be a powerful argument for thinking that, despite everything, they are useful words. Here is Dylan Thomas, for example, writing to his friend Henry Treece:

> I make one image—though 'make' is not the word; I let, perhaps, an image be 'made' emotionally in me and then apply to it what intellectual and critical forces I possess; let it breed another, let that image contradict the first; make of the third image, bred out of the other two together, a fourth contradictory image, and let them all, within my imposed formal limits, conflict. Each image holds within it the seed of its own destruction, and my dialectical method, as I understand it, is a constant building up and breaking down of the images that come out of the central seed, which is itself destructive and constructive at the same time . . . Out of the inevitable conflict of images—inevitable, because of the creative, recreative, destructive and contradictory nature of the motivating centre, the womb of war—I try to make that momentary peace which is a poem.[11]

These are strongly felt words. However, a queer light is thrown on them when you compare them with his practice. For the point about the metaphors in his poem 'If my head hurt a hair's foot':

'If my head hurt a hair's foot
Pack back the downed bone. If the unpricked ball of my breath
Bump on a spout let the bubbles jump out.
Sooner drop with the worm of the ropes round my throat
Than bully ill love in the clouted scene. . . .'

is that you are not able to realise them at all, nor are you meant to. They are *almost* entirely suggested by verbal associations (the first line plays on 'head of hair' and the pun hair/hare etc). Not *entirely* so; the poem, which I think is rather a fine one, exists in the narrowest possible margin between directed and fortuitous discourse. And though it is crammed with 'things' and with metaphors or (perhaps because of it) these have only the most flickering existence. The sense of vigour springs mainly not from realised metaphors but from the wrenched syntax, striking acoustic effects and hypnotic rhythm. And the effect is to reduce all 'things', whether they are named as part of a metaphor or for their own sake, to the same level. There is a 'thing'—something 'concrete'—in every foot, and this regular succession of 'things' comes to look, more than anything, like a form of *metre*. The conception of 'images' which Dylan Thomas expresses in the passage to Treece leads to a very special—very formal and verbalistic—type of poetry.

5

IDOLS AND WORLDS

1 IDOLS

Of course it is not surprising a cloud of half-formed meanings should hang round the word 'image'. There is an obvious reason in that so much of the language of mental operations (for reasons which I've suggested on pages 20–22) is taken from the eye and from sight. We 'imagine', we 'reflect', we 'speculate' (from Latin *specere*, to see); we have 'ideas' (from Greek *ἰδεῖν*, to see) and 'vision' and 'intuitions' (from Latin *intueri*, to look); ideas have 'brilliance', 'lucidity' or 'clarity', or are 'dazzling', and so on. No wonder if in grappling with the word 'image' we keep feeling we are tumbling from level to level of metaphor.

The word 'imagination', in particular, has always kept a vivid recollection of its etymology and carries with it the notion of making or receiving 'images'; and in most theories of the Imagination there is both an epistemological and a magical element. We tend, in thinking about the Imagination, to have the word 'images' in mind in two quite different senses: as optical perceptions, or the way the mind operates on such perceptions; and as *idols*—graven images or symbols which can draw down supernatural forces into themselves.

This is brought out clearly by Frances Yates in her remarkable book *The Art of Memory* (1966). She traces the history of a certain mnemonic art (traditionally invented by Simonides of Ceos, and popularised by Cicero, Quintilian and others) by which an orator was supposed to be able to help himself to commit things and words to memory by first memorising a place (for instance, cloisters with many arches, or a house with many rooms) and then, in imagination, placing mnemonic or symbolic 'images' on the 'places' he had memorised. The art of the 'artificial memory' was kept up by the medieval schoolmen, who adapted it to devotional purposes, and taken over by

Renaissance philosophers for quite different purposes again—magical ones. Giordano Bruno's treatises, ostensibly on the classical technique of the artificial memory, are actually, according to Frances Yates, heretical declarations of the magical and divine power of the Imagination to control the universe, by the manipulation of 'images' and 'places'.

Bruno held that the source of the poet's power was close to that of the painter (and of the philosopher too).

> Whence philosophers are in some ways painters and poets; poets are painters and philosophers; painters are philosophers and poets. Whence true poets, true painters, and true philosophers seek one another out and admire one another.[1]

It is not altogether an accident that the two themes—the analogy between poetry and the plastic arts; and the art of memory—have come together for us. Frances Yates remarks:

> To come upon the equation of poetry with painting in the context of the images of the art of memory reminds one, that according to Plutarch, it was Simonides, the inventor of the art of memory, who was the first to make this comparison.[2]

Bruno himself, however, is thinking of Horace's famous tag *ut pictura poesis* ('as is painting, so is poetry'), which was the basis of Renaissance theories of poetry and painting. The history of this dictum is actually rather odd—indeed if you were to think of it in relation to Horace himself, you would have to call it a mare's nest; for he was not really drawing any general comparison between poetry and painting at all—he was merely making the rather uninteresting remark that some poems, like some paintings, are best looked at from a distance whilst others can bear close inspection. Frances Yates, however, makes a good case for regarding Bruno, with his eloquent prescriptions for the construction of magical mental images or Phidias-like mental sculptures, as being—at least potentially—one of the great Renaissance artists. Moreover his theory of the *phantastica virtus* or power of fantasy, which is very close in some ways to the Romantic theory of the Imagination, was immediately recognised by his Puritan opponents as recommending *idolatry*. The controversy has some significance for literary history. As Frances Yates puts it:

A dilemma was presented to the Elizabethans in this debate . . . Either the inner images are to be totally removed by the Ramist method* or they are to be magically developed into the sole instruments for the grasp of reality. Either the corporeal similitudes of medieval piety are to be smashed or they are to be transposed into vast figures formed by Zeuxis and Phidias, the Renaissance artists of the fantasy. May not the urgency, and the agony of this conflict have helped to precipitate the emergence of Shakespeare?[3]

But what I think one feels about the example of Bruno is a pathos in that 'potentially'. For if Bruno was, as Frances Yates certainly persuades us, another Botticelli or Michelangelo, he was a Botticelli or Michelangelo inevitably manqué. He was deceived on a vast scale by a false analogy between literature and the plastic arts, and was trying to do in words what cannot be done. He was as doomed to failure in his artistic emulation of Zeuxis and Phidias as in his magical emulation of the Magus Hermes Trismegistus.

But a further point needs to be remembered about the background of the word 'image', as a literary term. There is a tradition going back to Aristotle according to which mental images are the very substance of thinking (*De anima*, 431a, 17: 'to think is to speculate with images'). And as a result of this it has been natural—though Ryle has shown it to be unnecessary—to consider that there must be some 'theatre' in which you view these images. And if it is as a spectacle in this inner theatre that we observe the world, it is equally natural to think of the 'theatre' as a 'world' in iself—the human mind as a smaller world, or microcosm, reflecting the larger world, or macrocosm. Mind, Theatre and World have constantly been linked by metaphor, and—as Frances Yates has shown—in magical belief. In Shakespeare's Globe Theatre, the name of which is itself significant, the stage represented the world, and the canopy, painted with heavenly bodies, was known as the 'Heavens'. Further, there were Renaissance exponents of the magical art of memory who actually built theatres of memory in wood and stone. The spectator, in these theatres, taking his stand on the stage, gazed round at a hierarchy of painted talismanic

* Ramus's method had no use for the old 'images' and 'places'.

images, arranged on the rising grades of the auditorium—and thereby was supposedly enabled to 'read off' and master the whole contents of the universe.[4]

I think this helps to explain the fact, which is very noticeable, that the words 'image' and 'world' tend to go together in the minds of literary critics: for instance, in the title of Donald Stauffer's book *Shakespeare's World of Images* (N.Y., 1949) or of an article by R. W. Short, 'Henry James's World of Images'.[5] The point is that, if you talk about 'images' in a work of literature (as opposed, say, to 'metaphors' or 'allusions') you find you need some receptacle or medium for the 'images' to exist or swim in. For there is some implication of autonomous existence in the word 'image' not present in 'metaphor' or 'allusion'. 'Images' suggest a race of independently existing organisms, which require a special habitat; and for this the most obvious candidate, recommended by both the epistemological and the magical traditions, is 'world'. And once you begin thinking of 'worlds', they always multiply; so that you are led on to the idea that if an author's 'images' compose a 'world', this must be part of another and larger world, the 'world of Henry James'. And the 'images' then have to be thought of as forming a world-within-a-world, a supposititious work of art within the work of art.

This tendency which studying 'images' has to make you also think about 'worlds' is very plain in Short's article. The article, anyway, is full of the puzzles you meet with in studies of 'imagery'. In his opening sentence, Short quotes Josephine Miles's warning: 'If the problem [of imagery] is subjective, how can it result in tables and charts?'[6] None the less, the counting and charting goes on merrily: '. . . perhaps no more than a quarter of the light-dark or height-depth images show the livelier qualities'; 'Redness and red objects are mentioned eleven times, for James a rather unusual insistence upon one colour'. And some of the things Short chooses to call 'images' seem even weirder than usual. James has a passage in *The Golden Bowl* about the purposes for which the Prince resorts to different languages—he speaks English when he wants to present himself as a good husband and son-in-law, French in his 'worse' moods etc. Short calls this an 'image-sequence'. He also wants to call the dinners and teas in Henry James 'images'. James, as he rightly points out, has a trick of mentioning meals and meal-times before we have been told whether it is day or night, and these meals 'may be called images because they are time-pegs, their bare unexploited names filling this extra function'.

From the study of the various 'image-areas' in James's work (already we are beginning to get the language of 'mapping') he says there will emerge 'lineaments of a cosmology, which could be combined with evidence from other sources to make a full account of the James world'. And he soon comes across 'image sequences' which not only cross the frontiers of the separate novels of James, making the different novels into parts of a larger 'world', but also form a 'world' or 'cosmogony' in themselves.

> When an image of the kind that is endued in use with momentary life is used over and over again, it picks up some added dimension of richness, begins to create its own peculiar myth, bridging not only its own separate uses but the author's separate works. And images of this kind reach out to others, even to those of unlike substance, in cosmogonal effect.[7]

And with this there begins the process, which we have noticed already in Clemen and others, of rejecting the work of art in favour of something else—converting it from a living organism into an inert mass of evidence, which can be 'mapped' and 'charted', and dismembered and re-assembled differently, at will.

'World' and 'image' are words that tend to be used in much the same sort of way. They are both useful for smuggling in the sense of *wholeness*. They are words you can fall back on when you want to persuade yourself, or your reader, that you have identified an entity, when actually you haven't. The words suggest that you are drawing a circle round something, but leave it to the listener to decide what. We come back to the business of 'mental images' here. For, since an actual optical image—the sort of picture you form when you look about you in daily life—is bound to be a whole, since it represents your whole field of vision, you tend to attribute the same quality to 'mental images'. You feel them to be wholes, however much or little there is in them. This tacit analogy with mental images gives the word 'image' a queer power to, as it were, fill up any space in a sentence that it occupies. Think, for instance, of what happens if you read an advertisement for an exhibition called 'An Image of Chile'. You guess that if you go to the exhibition you will see a lot of pictures or 'images' (most likely photographs) of Chile —together, perhaps, with some Chilean *objets d'art*, examples of local costume, a Chilean plough or two and so on. But you understand also that, however small or large the exhibition, you will be expected not to feel cheated by its title. It is up to you, as much as to the sponsors of the exhibition, to create a *whole* out of what you see. You will be expected to paper over the gaps and cracks—to accept the various objects and 'images' as adding up to a larger, comprehensive 'image', an epitome of the whole of Chile. And take away certain of the exhibits and the same would be true—you would still be expected to feel that the whole of Chile was somehow on show.

'Image' is a word that leaves most of the hard work to the reader; and so, even more, is 'world'. This is the point, therefore, to say a little more about this word, which is equally slippery, and causes the same kind of trouble in the criticism of fiction as the word 'image' does in that of poetry.

2 'WORLDS'

How true it is, I often tell myself, that when I arrive by an unfamiliar train at a part of England that is new to me, I cannot prevent one part of my mind suggesting that the people there are absolutely foreign. I see the same jeans, and kaftans and navy-blue suits over green pullovers, and I know what attitude I usually have to them, but I cannot call on these for the moment. If I talk to people on the train or in the street, shyness can make me feel like a stranger hurled from a different planet, only barely able, by a huge effort of translation, to make my needs known to them. For the moment, I have converted my surroundings into a brand-new, foreign and self-contained whole, which I am tempted to call a 'world'.

Again, when I come to the *same* place, a place that I know, like a part of London, by a different route or in a different context of events, something opposite but similar takes place. I push out of a crowded restaurant late in the evening into a Soho street, and I suddenly realise it is the same street which I visit every day at lunch-time. But I say to myself, puzzled: 'This is where I feel so-and-so, surely? And now to be expected to feel something quite different. I don't know how I'm going to do it.' It is like seeing the same set of illustrations attached to different books. And I try out which is best, whether to prolong my present state of feeling, and paint the scene anew with it, or go back to my lunchtime feelings which have tradition to support them. There seems no way of amalgamating the two experiences.

It is the same with our dealings with our friends. For some of us there is no worse nightmare than that all of our friends should be brought together in one room. 'They belong to different worlds,' we say to ourselves. It is not merely that the friends wouldn't get on. It is that we feel that if they came together we ourselves should burst to pieces, as the separate selves which we have created fought to occupy the same body at the same moment.

Everybody has these various experiences from time to time, I think. They were ones to which Proust attributed great significance. There is a passage in *The Guermantes Way* in which, to the eyes of the youthful narrator, the Princesse de Guermantes and her friends in their box at the Opéra seem so many marine deities, composed of, and inhabiting, an element different in every atom of its substance from that of the remainder of the audience. They swim in a 'sombre and transparent kingdom', bounded by their eyeballs—from which he has no more right than a stone or mineral to expect any sign of human recognition.

Again it was cardinal for the narrator in *Swann's Way* that nothing could ever bridge the gulf, the essential and unresolvable difference, between the Méséglise (or Swann's) Way and the Guermantes Way. They were 'sealed vessels' between which there could be no communication.

> I had invested each of them, by conceiving them in this way as two distinct entities, with that cohesion, that unity which belongs only to the figments of the mind; the smallest detail of either of them appeared to me as a precious thing, which exhibited the special excellence of the whole . . . I set between them, far more distinctly than the mere distances in miles and yards and inches which separated one from the other, the distance that there was between the two parts of my brain in which I used to think of them, one of those distances of the mind which time serves only to lengthen,

> which separate things irremediably from one another, keeping them for ever upon different planes.[8]

The remainder of *Remembrance of Things Past*, though, shows the narrator gradually discovering that the 'sealed vessels' do, after all, communicate. Time and time again he discovers that social 'worlds' which he had supposed mutually exclusive touch and overlap, thus ceasing to be 'worlds'. Indeed it was his acquaintance with Swann (and thus, in a sense, Swann's Way) which led him, circuitously, to the inaccessible kingdom of the Guermantes. Finally, in *Time Regained*, at the moment when he is about to be introduced to Gilberte's daughter (the fruit of the union of the Swann and Guermantes clans) he realises that, like a crossways in a forest, she represents the meeting-point not only of the Méséglise and Guermantes Ways but of innumerable other 'Ways'. 'Certainly, if only our hearts were in question,' he reflects, 'the poet was right when he spoke of the mysterious threads which life breaks.'

> But it is still truer that life is ceaselessly weaving them between beings, between events, that it crosses those threads, that it doubles them to thicken the woof with such industry that between the smallest point in our past and all the rest, the store of memories is so rich that only the choice of communications remains.[9]

One of the things common to all the phenomena I have been describing (and which one can call thinking in 'worlds') is that they are irrational. They represent a primitive and prerational mode of thought, one which reappears under all kinds of disguises, some beneficent and some pernicious. Proust saw that, in his own case, it underlay his profoundest insights and his grossest delusions. It was for him an essential factor in imaginative creation, and equally, in his social existence, it was the very basis of his snobbery. And one should remember that it is a kind of thinking which finds a natural expression in anti-Semitism. As Sartre points out in his *Reflections on the Jewish Question*, it is an essential part of the mythology of anti-Semitism (a mythology which Jews often subscribe to themselves) that any resemblance between the things a Jew does or possesses and their Aryan counterpart is illusory. A Jew's culture, his success, his love are only 'Jewish' culture, Jewish success and Jewish love—a sort of fairy gold, not to be confused with the real thing. Living in the midst of Aryan society, and to outward appearances a full member of it, he is for ever shut out from its 'real' existence. He inhabits a 'world' which coincides physically with the world of his Aryan neighbours but brings him no nearer to participation in it.

And what has to be said about all such convictions is that the person entertaining them *knows better*. He knows, with the rational part of his mind, that the Princesse de Guermantes is made of the same material as the people in the stalls and the gallery. Thinking in 'worlds' is only respectable when you remember that it is a paradox. And when people, when critics and journalists especially, talk about 'worlds' literally and without irony, it is a sign that something is wrong. It represents either laziness of mind or some definite confusion.

It is clear that writers, at present, find it extremely convenient to talk about 'worlds'. The heading 'The World of Music' catches my eye in the newspaper; and the article begins 'There are not many composers whose world is so full and self-sufficient that one would choose to live in it cut off from outside contacts for long.' You read of 'The Impressionists and their world,' 'The world of that Barrault film *Les Enfants du Paradis*.' 'The world of Japanese woodcuts' or 'The world of Truman Capote,' 'The ideal machinery of the Tridentine world' or *Shakespeare's World of Images*. I feel distrustful of so many worlds being discovered or created and suspect that entities are being multiplied needlessly. It is as if one were to go about founding innumerable exclusive but illusory clubs which never attain definite premises or a settled membership but exist ever afterwards as a name in the directory. No-one seems to have much use for these worlds after the moment of their creation. They are like the 'world' I create, out of shyness, on the train to Manchester, and promptly forget when my self-possession returns. And what they amount to is a deliberate act of laziness. Being unwilling to commit oneself to any noun of definite signification, however vague—even 'spirit' or 'ethos' would say too much—one falls back on a word which can be relied on to define nothing whatever and merely appears to draw a circle round the subject.

These are one of the two sorts of 'world' one is always meeting in literary journalism. And the other is the kind of 'world' which is meant when a critic says that a novelist 'creates his own world'. And the question in both cases is, why 'world'?

It is a favourite theory of reviewers and literary critics that a novelist should create a special fictional 'world'. 'Mr. Davidson', wrote Kathleen Nott in a novel-review, 'has created a genuine new world between American airfield and English harvest-field.' Here the word 'created' bears no great emphasis. She might as well have said that he 'found' this new world. She is talking the same language as those who speak of 'the world of Japanese woodcuts' or 'the world of Truman Capote'; she has invented a nonce world which will live for the space of an article and then return to limbo.

More often the theory includes the notion that the world is the novelist's own, a unique one, his particular speciality. 'With all her faults,' it often goes, 'we must admit that Miss — has done what stamps her as a true novelist; she has created her own strange yet utterly convincing world.' Lord David Cecil states it as a principle: 'A novel is a work of art in so far as it introduces us into a living world, in some respects resembling the world we live in, but with an individuality of its own.'

The novelist praised in this way is thought to secrete a certain unique colouring, of which he alone has the formula, and to impregnate his fictional 'world' with it.

> In three novels, Thomas Hinde has built up a world that is original and disturbing, and wholly his own. And the deadpan style, economical almost to the point of transparency at times, the description more by implication than by facts and adjectives, is all part of the pared-down feeling, the curious sense of waiting, of significance, of a sort of spiritual pregnancy. . . .

And as his 'world' is said to be 'wholly his own', so his characters are said to have 'a life of their own':

> Its characters [those of *The Snowman*, by Charles Haldeman] are either grotesques or fragmentary consciences for whose conduct we receive little guide from the progress of the plot. Yet they fasten hold of our imagination with a bizarre tenacity and a precise life of their own. Ambiguities occur mainly in the moral world in which Mr. Haldeman requires them to live and in the

images, like that of the snowman itself, by which he seeks to embody that world.'

Now I will say at once that I think the theory that a novelist should 'create his own world' is false. But what I am objecting to is not so much the idea of his creating a world as of its being his own. There is nothing wrong with saying, as Zola did, that Balzac created or fathered a world. 'Balzac remains for us, I repeat, a power not to be argued with. He imposes himself, like Shakespeare, by a creative *fiat* [*un souffle createur*] which has fathered a whole world.' What this means primarily is that Balzac rivalled God in inventive power. He put an extraordinary abundance, an awful lot of things, into the *Comédie humaine*. People do not, on the whole, say that Balzac created 'a world of his own'. The implication is that he seconded God's power, not that he constructed a rival creation to God's. If people do talk of the novels of Balzac (or Proust or Dickens) as rivalling the everyday world, all they mean is that they are tempted to sit reading them rather than make money or love on their own account.

Zola's remark can also be taken to mean—what is equally true—that Balzac aimed at getting the *whole* of something in, in his case the entirety of French society. It is something which became a much more precise ambition for the great post-Naturalist novelists. Proust and Joyce had a very clear determination to get the *whole* of something in—the whole of a single day in Dublin or the whole of one man's memories. The Naturalist novelists, like Zola and the Goncourts, by posing in the role of a scientist towards their material, were *ipso facto* prevented from depicting the whole of anything—for the whole of anything that is observed has to include the observer. The post-Naturalist novelists found the way on from Naturalism to lie in abolishing or incorporating the observer.

A further idea, however, comes into the talk of the novelist 'fathering' a world, the idea that he makes it a self-contained whole, that he gives it the unity and structure of a world. Frank Kermode, speaking of Lawrence, Forster and Joyce, wrote:

> They all saw the novel as a world, not in a trite sense, but with very exalted notions of what wholeness is. They hated divisions, whether between thought and emotion, sense and spirit, form and matter, pleasure and value . . .

> To make a world it is necessary, but not enough, to know this one; to bring its possibilities to being the artist has to put forth all his goodness. His world will have its myths, its politics, it sociology and psychology, as Pasternak's has; but it will never be devoted to illuminating their counterparts in life.[10]

The operative phrase is 'devoted to', of course; Kermode is warning us not to regard the novels of Lawrence and others as psychological or political treatises. All the same there is something paradoxical in this. *Aren't* the politics and the psychology in their novels devoted to illuminating their counterparts in life?

I think they are, and that the trouble arises from using the word 'world' in this way. For why 'world'? The world doesn't deserve the praise of being 'whole' and a 'unity'. It is whole and a unit only because it happens to be all there is—so that it would be illogical to accuse it of any deficiency. It hasn't 'a' structure, it has an infinity of possible structures. It is not a good metaphor for wholeness and oneness in the sense of symmetry and inner harmony—except for the fact that the earth, as opposed to the world, happens to be spherical.

Two quite different senses of the word 'world' have got mixed up here. For evidently, novels are about the world; that is to say, they are about life and the visible scene, as mathematics are not. And if you can get a great deal of reality and human multiplicity into your fiction, you can perfectly well be said to have created a world, as Zola said of Balzac. But on the other hand, novels are objects in themselves; they have parts and limbs; and these or their nice adjustment or organic relation to each other, make up what you can call an 'organic whole' or an 'aesthetic monad'. Or if you are Kermode, you may want to call it a 'world'. But 'world' in this sense has nothing to do with the other sense of 'world'—i.e. what the novel is about.

Kermode seems to me to mix up these two meanings. In talking of a novel, or any work of art, as an aesthetic object he would be happy, I think, to speak of it, in the usual Romantic and post-Romantic manner, as an 'organism'—meaning that, if it is a true work of art, its parts interpenetrate and form a unity possessing qualities not inherent in them separately. Only in the case of the novel he changes his metaphor from 'organism' to 'world'. And 'world' in this sense suggests a false connection with the 'world' that the novel is about.

The two senses of 'world' are not only different but contradictory—though also complementary. For viewed as an aesthetic object a novel or a play ought to be something self-enclosed and complete and internally harmonious, as should any work of art. But from the point of view of subject-matter it should have quite different qualities; it should be unenclosed, outward-looking and suggest endless perspectives. Henry James constantly came back to this distinction:

> . . . though the relations of a human figure or a social occurrence are what make such objects interesting, they also make them, to the same tune, difficult to isolate, to surround with the sharp black line, to frame in the square, the circle, the charming oval, that helps any arrangement of objects to become a picture . . . The play consents to the logic of but one way, mathematically right, and with the loose end as gross an impertinence on its surface, and as grave a dishonour, as the dangle of a snippet of silk or wool on the right side of a tapestry. We are shut up within the action itself; no part of which is related to anything but some other part—*save of course by the relation of the total to life.* (My italics)[11]

If you write about the world, you are writing about something which is sprawling, multiform and infinitely extensive. But if you say that a novelist creates his own 'strange yet convincing world', you mean he has created something insulated and isolated, like a knot in timber rather than a figure in the carpet—something very unlike *the* world, that is, but which will somehow provide a substitute. And it will be false or unsatisfying precisely in what James calls 'the relation of the total to life'.

What James means by 'the relation of the total to life' is no more predictable in the case of a novel than in that of a poem. There is no general rule about how novels, any more than poems, relate to life. Every achieved work of art is unique in the nature of its link with the real world. This is the most elusive, as it is the most important, thing about it.

Eliot, faithful to the doctrine of the 'objective correlative', always insisted that this 'relation of the total to life' must be left unstated. In literature, he says in his essay 'The Possibility of a Poetic Drama',[12] an idea 'can remain pure only by being stated simply in the form of a general truth, or by being transmuted, as the attitude of Flaubert towards the small bourgeois is transformed in *L'Education sentimentale.* It has become so identified with the reality that you can no longer say what the idea is.' The work of a novelist like Thackeray or a dramatist like Shaw or Goethe fails the test of art, he says, because it includes reflection—it is no longer pure 'presentation'. And he goes on: 'The essential is to get upon the stage this precise statement of life which is at the same time a point of view, a "world"—a world which the author's mind has subjected to a complete process of simplification.' In this sentence Eliot is holding the two senses in which a play or novel can be thought of as a 'world' beautifully distinct. In so far as it is *about* the world or life, it is a 'precise statement' of the world common to us all (not just the author's private one). But in its aspect as a work of art it is an independent 'world', completely malleable in the author's hands.

One should remember, though, that some novelists and playwrights deliberately exploit the 'impurity' of comment and reflection—they positively obtrude, or pretend to obtrude, the life outside the covers of the book or the confines of the stage. And whilst of course these authorly intrusions don't represent the *true* 'relation of the total to life'—and indeed because of that fact—they can play quite a subtle fictional role. The late W. J. Harvey brought this out well in regard to Fielding:

> . . . the novelist may so disguise the frontiers of his fiction that we sense beyond the story the continuum of life itself. In this way the reader's experience of fiction merges imperceptibly into other, 'real-life' experiences just as, in actuality, one context of our lives overlaps with another. This disguise, this effect of blurring the frontiers of fiction and life, is again the product of art, whether naive or crafty. A crude example, I think, is the technique of montage used by Dos Passos in *U.S.A.*; we may contrast with this the author's addresses to the reader in *Tom Jones*. These may look simple-minded when compared with modern technical experiments but are, I believe, sophisticated and designed to produce quite complicated effects upon the reader. At first sight they might seem to be conventional devices artificially

> delimiting the area of the novel. But they have the opposite effect, raising the novel to the magnitude of life itself and giving the fictional world a wonderful openness which is then played off against the formal intricacy of the plot.[13]

There is, perhaps, something which superficially reminds you of the talk of a novelist 'creating his own world' in the attitude of the Symbolist poet, who felt that his poem was an autonomous object, an 'aesthetic monad', out of the flux of life and with no connection with utility or discursive reasoning. But if you talk about a novel in this way, you must be talking of what it has in common with a Symbolist poem—you will be talking of its qualities as an aesthetic object, not of what it's about; and in this sense any true work of art should be 'a world of its own'.—The other strand of the Symbolist tradition puts us right. For whereas, as Frank Kermode has pointed out, the artist in this tradition feels that to create a work of art he has to cut himself off from the common human satisfactions, to turn himself into a homeless wanderer with nowhere to lay his head, he also has no place *in* the 'world' he has created, any more than any other breathing and existing thing. The work of art, by its very nature, denies and excludes his humanity; it is as far as possible from being 'his own, unique world'. It is not there to satisfy his personal desires. It is no private sanctuary for him, which is what is implied by saying a novelist 'creates a world of his own'. On the contrary he stands aloof from it, 'refined out of existence, indifferent, paring his fingernails'. It is on this understanding that the work of art is able to illuminate real life.

All the same, when a reviewer says that so-and-so's novel 'creates its own world', it is often a genuine reaction. Only he is using the wrong metaphor. What he means is not that the novelist is creating some rival to the real world, but that he is fencing off a part of the real world, with himself inside it, and converting it into a playground where he can erect follies and rearrange Nature as it pleases him. It is very true that some novelists do this; and that is what is wrong with them. For it is easy enough to make your own world if you falsify the real world to do it. When a novel gets praised in this way, it is often a hint that something has gone wrong. In the case of a true novel, however small its chosen area, life, reality and the world stretch round it and you feel them there; nothing is excluded by the narrowness of the point of focus. But, with another sort of novel, you feel that the author is not bringing all he knows to bear on what he is writing. He *knows better*. He is secluding some part of himself from the reader; there has not been the collision of a complete personality with something taken whole from life; and the book, as a consequence, though it may have brilliant qualities, is cut-off, self-enclosed and non-conductive.

For instance, there is the novelist who is said to recreate childhood (a 'child's world') with astonishing fidelity. The reviewer praises his novel, and yet he is not really happy about it. He calls it a 'tour de force', which immediately puts it in its place; and he may go on to grumble that there have been too many novels doing the same thing—except that this one is different. What in fact is likely to be wrong with the novel is that adult knowledge has not been brought to bear on the childhood experience. Think of L. P. Hartley's *The Go-between*. It was nearly a very distinguished novel. It *was* a distinguished novel at the moments when, in rendering the boy's experience, it rendered at the same time the emotions, of beguilement and horror and rueful hindsight, with which this experience returned to the middle-aged narrator's mind. It was essential to dramatise the narrator as well as the boy; the novel existed in the interplay between them, and it was by this perspective that it led out into the world at large—this was the 'relation to the total of life'. For whole long stretches, however—for instance the scene of the cricket-match—all you get is the boy's experience (or 'world'). The novel thins out at these points, so that it remains only a sketch of the fine novel it might have been.

Something like this is true of Iris Murdoch. Her novels tend to begin very substantially, with figures solidly placed in a background and standing in the light of day, with human possibilities and perspectives stretching round them as far as the eye can see. Then the shutters come down, the theatre-exits are closed, and the characters fall into their dance; the thing becomes a ballet of bloodless essences, in which characters act out their feelings over-literally—choreographically as it were. Her people strike us as less solid and less rich at the end of her novels than they do at the beginning. A kind of falsity has set in as soon as the novel turns into 'a world of its own'.

Would not Ivy Compton-Burnett be another case in point, and a particularly interesting one? She strikes me as having, with a cheerful cynicism towards the pretensions of the novel, deliberately elected to convert a piece of the real world into 'a world of her own'. In her novels the shutters are down from the beginning. She is peculiarly a novelist who draws a circle and says, 'beyond that I shall not look'. And it's in vain for us to look, either. Her characters materialise out of a void. One feels the presence of nothing outside the circle she has drawn, that country household in 1910; and what we find within it, not surprisingly, varies wildly in its credibility. There is some solidity and depth of observation behind her gallery of domestic tyrants, but the purest Wodehousian fantasy when it comes to her butlers. Her plots, as Charles Burkhart admits it in his eulogistic book about her,[14] are 'servantlike', and her cynicism about the novel comes out in what she once said about them: 'As regards plots I find real life no help at all. Real life seems to have no plots, and as I think a plot desirable and almost necessary, I have this extra grudge against life.' It hardly seems to matter, so much has she insulated the 'world' of her novels for her own end, i.e. the practice of a certain kind of wit. And this is not to denigrate her. Her wit is a marvellous, superior, intelligent pleasure. She is a *philosophe*, a wit of the anti-Victorian school of Butler, Shaw and Wilde, who has pitched her tent in the field of fiction and made herself as snug there as possible. Pit her against her fellow *philosophes* and she shines. It is only when you compare her, as critics have sometimes done, with Jane Austen and Henry James that it appears how little you compliment a novelist by saying he 'creates his own world'.

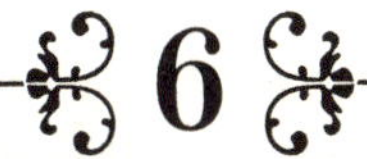

'THE IDEAL'

There is a further and final point to be made. All the ways of thinking I have been talking about—wanting words to 'come true' and *be* the thing they refer to; wanting metaphors to 'come true' and take on the quality of existence, losing their duality and becoming 'images'; and discussing literature in terms of 'worlds'—ought to be thought of in an even wider context: I mean the general distrust in twentieth-century thought of dualisms of every kind.

One name to give to this is the decline of the notion of the 'ideal'. It means talking rather impressionistically and clumsily to make the point; but though the nineteenth century was the heyday of the *word* 'ideal', I think you might say it marked the death of the feeling the word stood for. There was, in all previous Western high culture, a sense for a sphere, or realm, or world (but all the words are bad), which was the antithesis of the human and served as a term of reference for it—a sense for heaven, in fact: the gold heaven, not the blue. This serene and radiant region was out the sphere of time and accident, the antitype of human desire and appetite. It was the abode of criteria and patterns, neither abetting human activity nor in conflict with it, but existing as its permanent and regulating opposite—no more necessarily at odds with human action, you might say, than a frame is at odds with a painting. It was that which all ceremony and art assumed instinctively as their final point of reference, so that art would always be better than life. And it was, in a sense, the same conception, this 'ideal', it was the same habit of mind, whether supported by metaphysical theory, as in Platonic Idealism, or given symbolic embodiment, as in Christian mythology, or codified, as in Augustan social and literary canons.

This consciousness of the 'ideal' went with traditionalism and was supported by the notion of hierarchy—whether the hierarchy of the literary genres, by which one style was regarded as suitable for one kind of subject-matter and another for another, or the ideas of social hierarchy underlying this. And one of the most pervasive results of the revolutions of the first part of the nineteenth century—the industrial, the French and scientific revolutions, the Romantic revival (with its unsettling of literary genres), the assault on the Bible, and so on, was not merely to shake the assumptions underlying 'the ideal' but to destroy the living sense of it. Nineteenth-century writers and philosophers talked enormously about the 'ideal',* but as a habit of mind it was actually dying.†

It is interesting to see such a representative nineteenth-century figure as Ruskin coping with the word in *Modern Painters.* With his usual honesty he admits that it bothers him. The trouble arises, he says, from the 'unfortunate distinction between Idealism and Realism which leads most people to imagine the Ideal opposed to the Real, and therefore *false*'. There are, he says, two senses in which the word 'ideal' is used. In one sense, any work of art which represents not a material object but the mental conception of a material object, can be called 'ideal'; that is to say, it represents an idea and not a thing. But there is another sense, in which the form of a Caliban can be said to be less 'ideal' than that of an Antinous, because the latter is nearer the general conception of the human *species.* This second sense is an awkward one, he thinks, because (the word 'ideal' also having the connotation of 'imaginary', i.e. *un*real) it seems to imply that no ideal or perfect example of a given species can ever actually exist. Whereas, if you consider the oyster or the primrose, you have to admit that many oysters and primroses, of full size and healthy condition, are as perfect specimens as you could wish for, and however much we combined the features of two or more of them, we couldn't produce a better one. Trees are in a slightly different case, as they often have to grow in what are, from their point of view, very uncomfortable situations.

---

* As of course did eighteenth-century writers too; in particular in the controversy centring upon Reynolds and the *beau idéal* in painting.

† The shift in the sense of the word 'normal' (as in 'Ecole normale') from 'representing a pattern of excellence' to 'average' obviously represents something similar.

Now it would be hard upon the plant, if, after being tied to a particular spot, where it is indeed much wanted, and is a great blessing, but where it has enough to do to live; whence it cannot move to obtain what it needs or likes, but must stretch its unfortunate arms here and there for bare breath and light, and split its way among rocks, and grope for sustenance in unkindly soil; it would be hard upon the plant, I say, if under all these disadvantages, it were made answerable for its appearance, and found fault with because it was not a fine plant of the kind . . .

So then there is in trees no perfect form which can be fixed upon or reasoned out as ideal; but that is always an ideal oak which, however poverty-stricken, or hunger-pinched, or tempest-tortured, is yet seen to have done, under its appointed circumstances, all that could be expected of oak.[1]

And if we ask, he says, how he reconciles this definition of ideality with what he has said elsewhere about the connection between beauty in living organisms and an appearance of *happiness*,

let it be observed, and for ever held, that the right and true happiness of every creature is in this very discharge of its function, and in those efforts by which its strength and inherent energy are developed.[2]

(Here, of course his aesthetic theories are pointing the way towards his political and economic ones.)

Ruskin's notion of the 'ideal', in so far as he is serious about it at all, is strangely utilitarian and naturalistic—a sort of vote of thanks, for doing his best in all circumstances, to a member of a firm of which Man is chief shareholder and God the managing director. He thinks of 'the ideal' as something which can be, and often is, attained. Whereas, according to the older habit of thought, there could be no question of attaining (or of failing to attain) the ideal: it was not that sort of relationship. And indeed there was no place in Ruskin's vision of the world—a supremely beautiful world, composed by a near, visible and beneficent Deity, in a chordal unity of innumerable exquisite species, each fitted to further Man's moral progress—for anything so foreign, and opposed to Nature, as the older 'ideal'.

One way of thinking of 'the ideal' is as a frame—for instance, the gilded picture-frame. The type of picture-frame familiar to us is not a very old invention. It came in at the Renaissance, when painting moved out of the church, where it had its own architectural setting, onto the walls of secular apartments. But for three centuries and more the picture-frame, with its 'heavenly' gilding (preserving an echo of the golden ground of pre-Renaissance painting) served, in a small way, some of the regulatory function of 'the ideal'. Mannerist and baroque painters might sometimes playfully break the frame, allowing Neptune or Venus to extend a foreshortened leg into the *grand salon*; but it was not till the time of the Impressionists that there was a serious and deliberate revolt against its authority. The Impressionists began by abandoning the heavy carved gilt frame for the 'philosophically white and abstract'[3] kind. They did so from a mixture of motives: it was partly a technical matter, for gold is destructive of orange tone; and partly, no doubt, a matter of democratic dislike of the flavour of ostentation and possession. But their revolt also reflected a general reaction against ornament; and the rejection of ornament in art is in itself not merely a rejection of a debased artistic tradition but a case of turning away from 'the ideal' in general. Seurat then went further, and spotted his white frames with variable colour, in accordance with the imaginary direction of the sunlight in the picture, so creating the fiction that the frame was actually there in the observed scene. And by this time a feeling of rebellion against the frame seems to have become widespread, and painters even began to exhibit unframed canvases.

I think of this as a kind of allegory of something larger, which you might likewise call 'abolishing the frame', and which has been a main trend of the present century. The examples are innumerable, and we find them in evey sort of context. For instance, the way that, through the influence of the Bauhaus, typography has been liberated from its ornamental and regulatory conventions: its 'monarchical' upper-case letters, its ornamental serifs and (as far as possible) punctuation. Or the way book-illustrations learned to 'bleed', as if wanting to rejoin the world, and photographers to try to catch the sitter with ruffled hair or smoking; or the way, in the twentieth century, plays began to break down the distinction between actors and audience, and the plastic arts to break down the barriers between art and reality.

Clearly, in a sense, this trend is a fruit of the great nineteenth-century revolutions. It contains a strong element of democratic egalitarianism, both in its political and its artistic forms. It looks back to Romanticism, with its revolt against the aristocratic idols in art, the 'cold formalities' which imprison the human heart, and to Realism and Naturalism, with their revolt against the bourgeois idols.

But I think you cannot interpret this 'abolishing the frame' in the twentieth century as just a pulling down of idols or as the echo of past revolutions—for in this case it would produce diminishing returns, and its work would fairly soon be over. It has to be seen as something more absolute. It reflects something new, a major discovery of the early twentieth century rather than the nineteenth century, and one to which many trails lead. There have been many different twentieth-century revolutions, but they seem to have had a common signature: the recognition not only that traditional standards of reference have to be abandoned, but that there is something wrong with the whole *idea* of standards of reference.

To put it as crudely as possible, hitherto the normal assumption in approaching speculative questions was that you measured one thing against another—this other, the criterion, being, for the moment, left more or less unexamined and assumed to be understood or immutable. It is this point of reference, or criterion, which came under suspicion as a false 'metaphysical' habit of thought. Linguistic philosophers were forced to conclude that there was only one legitimate subject of philosophical enquiry, the way people do in fact use language; whilst the school of Husserl and the phenomenologists claimed the sole aim of philosophy to be *description*. Linguists decisively rejected the notion of 'correctness' in language and came to see their business as the impartial study of usage.* Whilst historians of

* 'We have seen . . . that may people's notion of correct English is based, not on the actual *usage* of any section of the population, but on a sort of "transcendental" standard which is essentially an amalgam of logic and the grammar of the classical languages. Thus certain forms are held to be "correct" which are rarely, if ever, used at all; while many other forms, although they are in common use even among educated people, are condemned as "incorrect".

'These misconceptions are usually acquired, or imposed, at a highly impressionable age, and those who hold them will generally the Namier school came to feel that the task of history-writing was to reject inappropriate 'universals', and to translate public events out of the notional shadow-play of movements and generalities into the precise and concrete terms of the acts of individuals—the 'innumerable acts of innumerable persons'.

This, after all, was what it meant to be living in the 'positivist' age, and it is not just sentimental to call the age by this name. The third stage in human progress announced by Comte in his *Philosophie positive* had really arrived: it had to be taken for granted—with whatever exhilaration, sense of desolation or indifference—that we were now left alone, all metaphysical ghosts laid, with *things*, or 'things as they are', and could make use of no traditional frames to look at them through. The nearest one could allow oneself to a frame was a 'model', a criterion which one deliberately constructed for one's own specific purposes. And any thinker in the 'positivist' age had therefore to adopt a humbler attitude towards phenomena—something, say, on the lines of Bergson's 'intuition', by which we put aside abstract concepts (the 'broken fragments of reality') and immerse ourselves in the living flux; or the anti-interpretative attitude of Merleau-Ponty.

> There cannot be one absolute meaning for existence, since that presumes the intellectualist distinction between transcendent meaning and human existence that Merleau-Ponty decries. His writing does not *interpret* in the usual sense, for then it would have to be *about* something; rather, it is already in the dimension of meaning ('we are condemned to meaning') and its primary job is the articulation of that already present immanence. Not how the world is but that it is . . .[4]

There were two main ways in which the artist initially reacted to the need to say farewell to criteria. He tried to produce the kind of work of art which contained its own criteria within it; this was the Symbolist doctrine, or one aspect of it: the theory of the work of art as 'intensive manifold', self-sufficient and not dependent on the world at large, and excluding even the artist himself. Or alternatively he decided that the frontiers between

---

assume their truth to be self-evident.' (Jeremy Warburg, 'Notions of Correctness', in Randolph Quirk's *The Use of English*, 1962, pp. 325–6.)

his own art and the other arts, between the practical arts and the fine arts, and between the arts and life itself, must be broken down, in the interests of a new unity.

These two reactions, which in most respects were contrary to each other, agreed in breaking with the dualistic habit of mind. They abandoned the traditional notion of art as the interplay between a content and a pre-established mould or between a chosen block of reality and a detached observer. Both reactions aimed at unity and singleness, whether the desperate unity of the Hermetic and self-contained Symbolist art-work (or 'world'), or the joyful unity of all human energies and faculties envisaged by Gropius:

> The dominant spirit of our epoch is already recognisable although its form is not yet clearly defined. The old dualistic world-concept which envisages the ego in opposition to the universe is rapidly losing ground. In its place is rising the idea of a universal unity in which all opposing forces exist in a state of absolute balance. This dawning recognition of the essential oneness of all things and their appearances endows creative effort with a fundamental inner meaning. No longer can anything exist in isolation. We perceive every form as the embodiment of an idea, every piece of work as a manifestation of our innermost selves.[5]

It is significant that Symbolist theorists give a new sense to 'outline' in works of art. For 'outline' has one sense if you think of a work as outlining itself against some other complementary thing, a background or a heaven, and quite another if all it has to outline itself against is indiscriminate flux or howling emptiness. So Yeats, in commenting on Blake's remark that 'The great and golden rule of art, as of life, is this: that the more distinct, sharp and wiry the boundary-line, the more perfect the work of art', explains 'He does not mean by outline the bounding-line dividing a form from its background . . . but the line that divides it from surrounding space.' And something of the same sort is implied when Joyce makes Stephen Dedalus speak of the 'aesthetic image' as 'first luminously apprehended as self-bounded and self-contained upon the immeasurable background of space or time which is not it'.

The tone of the Symbolists in this anti-dualistic way of talking is a stoical and suffering one, as against the buoyant utopian note of the Bauhaus. And, historically speaking, the second doctrine came as a reaction against the first. But both had roots in the sense of social impotence and isolation felt by artists in the mid-nineteenth century, and were, in the one case, a decision defiantly to accept and deepen this isolation, accepting all its consequences, even in the form of 'despondency and madness', and in the other, to resist it at all costs. And indeed the Bauhaus doctrine was in some respects the older doctrine and drew on a continuous tradition of nineteenth-century thought. It had a warrant (appropriately, considering its first home in Weimar) in Goethe, who campaigned ceaselessly against the separation of the human faculties; and it took some of its impulse from William Morris, whose campaign to revitalise the practical arts went with a deep distrust of the exclusiveness of the fine arts. (Indeed, he was ready, in a quite nihilistic way, to sweep away traditional Western culture altogether as a source of barren separatism.)

In all this, it is worth pointing out that artistic theory was prophetic. 'Modernist' artistic thought was very quick to sense the larger implications of the nineteenth-century 'positivist' revolution, and in some ways 'modernist' artists became path-finders for other kinds of thinkers. For instance, Sorel's theory of revolution—the argument that it is wrong to formulate aims for a revolution, because if one could predict the consequences of a revolution, it would not *be* one—seems to have its roots in aesthetic theory: it was an extension of the Symbolist notion of words attracting a meaning to themselves only after they have been written.

The habit of thinking in terms of 'the ideal' and of dualistic conceptions is so deep-seated that the implications of questioning it take a lot of realising. We are still exploring them, and have a long way to go. However, Marshall McLuhan has pointed out one very likely reason why the task might be especially difficult—that the actual medium we use in communicating our ideas, the printed page, encourages us to cling to old habits of thought. I would like to digress a bit about McLuhan here. For both the weakness and the strength of his ideas are bound up with his doctrinaire anti-dualism. The weakness lies in the fact that, in order to persuade us that a radical change is taking place in the way we experience the universe, he writes in a style that presupposes the change has already happened. Thus, in arguing that the reign of print-culture is nearing its end, he already abandons the old-fashioned sequential reasoning associated with it and writes in a series of fragmentary propositions—these being supposed, through their multiple inter-connections, to assemble themselves into a 'configuration'. This really seems to be wish-fulfilment, and a kind of science-fiction. If you are intending to turn print against itself and disrupt the very habits of print-culture, you have at least got to draw on all its resources, including connected argument. In the same way, one of the main troubles the reader has with McLuhan is that he never knows if the daring connections that he makes are meant to be analogies or something more. But the point is, to his anti-dualistic turn of mind there is something anachronistic in the whole *idea* of an analogy. He feels it to be one of the dualistic notions left over from print-culture; and, for him, any analogy, if you stare at it hard enough, turns out to be an identity. This is the credulous side to McLuhan; and from this point of view the nearest thing to him is the writing of the Swedenborgians.*

On the other hand, one of his leaps of connection has real importance and is not merely credulous. He has seen that the revolutionary insights of modernist aesthetics are not just an arcane speciality but have significance for the world at large—a major step, considering the common cry against the exclusiveness of modern art. It is modernist literature which first became restless about print, with its rigid convention of 'one thing after another'. And certainly print and typography are one of the traditional 'frames' we have been talking about, and it is important to be as aware of this as possible. You need, if not to break this 'frame', at least to look round it. Likewise, a way of seeing things as, to use McLuhan's terms, a 'unified field' or a 'configuration' do seems to be what the anti-dualistic attitude and the impulse to 'break the frame' are leading towards. And if, as I've said earlier, this impulse is more absolute than any particular historic revolt or throwing-down of idols, it is also more intimate. You catch sight of it at work, out of the corner of your

---

* I am thinking of Henry James the elder's Swedenborgian friend J. Garth Wilkinson, author of *The Human Body and its Connexion with Man* (1851). Wilkinson writes as if, for instance, the European road-system not only showed a similarity to the human circulatory system but were actually, in some way, *the same thing*.

eye, in a hundred different connections—less as a 'trend' than as a fixed habit of mind, giving its own stamp to ways of thought in other respects quite opposite.

You might take as a simple example, the questioning of the whole traditional idea of an 'examination' in England today. The programme for the new Certificate of Secondary Education contains provisions for what you might call a 'criterion-less' examination—or what comes to almost the same thing, an examination which constructs a unique set of criteria for each candidate, in terms of the candidate's own projects and aims. The radical group in psychiatry attack the institution of the family along similar lines. The family is pernicious, argued David Cooper in a speech reported in the *Observer* of 2 March 1969, because it is the prime source of dualistic 'games'. He went on:

> The lethal qualities of the family are replicated in every other institution in our society—schools, businesses and social organisations. In all academic disciplines and in all institutions in capitalist society, as in the family, people played 'games' that had to be unlearnt.
>
> These games were those which worked on a 'binary role' system which is based on forced dualities, such as teacher and taught, doctor and patient, parent and child. In all these 'games' one person was defined as being 'up' or superior and the other as 'down' or inferior.

And one doesn't have to accept such extreme positions to admit that the habit of mind is a necessary one. The original, archetypal 'frame', the instinctive confidence in 'the ideal', having disappeared, you are bound to go on questioning every individual 'content and frame' or 'object and criterion' relationship, to try the effect of 'breaking the frame'. It is the rational thing to do; just as it is reasonable for people in this situation to look for support to philosophies, like Zen Buddhism and Taoism, which reconcile or abolish dualities.*

The poetic attitude of looking for truth and significance

* For is and is not come together;
Hard and easy are complementary;
Long and short are relative;
High and low are comparative; . . .
(Poem 2 of the *Tao Te Ching*, trans. R. Blakney, 1955.)

primarily in 'things', which we were talking about earlier, has a strong anti-dualistic aspect, in that it abolishes the idea of the poet as *set over against* things. One could find a symbol for this attitude in the popularity of the *Odyssey*, as opposed to the *Iliad*, in the twentieth century. The fact has certainly been rather striking. Two of the major 'modernist' works in English, *Ulysses* and the *Cantos*, used the Odyssey as framework; and a whole genre of shorter poems has grown up in the form of an offhand or allusive retelling of the Ulysses story.* The significance of this is at bottom philosophical. Ulysses is an admirable symbol for the man who takes the shapes of surrounding things and circumstances—anti-abstractionist man, refusing (unlike the heroes of the *Iliad*) to impose preconceived patterns or frames on things, the man willing to subdue himself to the material he works in, to respect the 'given' and wrap himself round its contours.

This interpretation of the Ulysses myth was deepened and refined by Pound in his notion of the 'periplus', on which Hugh Kenner has some remarkable pages in *The Poetry of Ezra Pound.*

> The word 'periplum', which recurs continually throughout the *Pisan Cantos,* is glossed in Canto LIX:
>
> periplum, not as land looks on a map
> but as sea bord seen by men sailing.
>
> Victor Bérard discovered that the geography of the *Odyssey*, grotesque when referred to a map, was minutely accurate according to the Phoenician voyagers' *periploi* . . . The periplum, the voyage of discovery among facts, whose tools is the ideogram, is everywhere contrasted with the conventions and the bird's eye view afforded by the map. Forms grow out of data. They are not imposed on data . . . The sense of intellectual adventure, the sense of fact, the sense of the intelligibility of assembled particulars, 'too

---

* Plenty of other examples come to mind. Kazantzakis's *magnum opus* was a vast *Odyssey*; and when Joyce arrived in Paris in 1920 with the manuscript of *Ulysses* he wrote to his brother Stanislaus: 'Odyssey very much in the air here. Anatole France is writing *Le Cyclops*, G. Fauré, the musician an opera *Penélopé*. Giraudoux has written *Elpenor* (Paddy Dignam). Guillaume Apollinaire *Les Mamelles de Tirésias*.' (25 July 1920).

necessary a conclusion from all the more intelligent activity of many decades for there to be the least question of its belonging to anyone in particular', comprises the *forma mentis* of ideogram and of the Cantos . . .[5]

It is one implication of this new monistic artistic attitude, and of the discipline of beginning from 'things', that the one abstraction which modernist writers freely allow themselves is 'life'. The grand effort of the modernist novelists, the thing for which we most of all prize them, is their heroic effort to identify 'life' itself—a protean entity, referrable to nothing outside itself, and taking shapes which, if one labels them 'flesh' or 'spirit', 'humility', or 'loyalty', or 'character', it is with the consciousness that all such names are provisional. There is this unobtrusive modernist side even to such a traditional novelist as Forster; and it is a dominating theme in Lawrence, Joyce and Virginia Woolf. Lawrence's modernity was to write of the feelings which have no name.

Another of the consequences of a habit of 'breaking the frame', for a thinker or artist, however, is to leave him uncertain how to propel himself into motion at all. To mix a metaphor, he misses the customary 'leverage' which frames provided. I take the word 'leverage' from Hugh Kenner, who uses it apropos of *vers libre.* One must not suppose, he says, that 'the essence of metric is a mechanical pattern from which dramatic deviations take place, and hence that *vers libre* is inherently lacking in leverage'. And it was against any such notion that rhythm had inevitably to be referred to a norm that Pound formulated his belief in 'absolute rhythm'—according to which 'every emotion and every phase of emotion has some toneless phrase, some rhythm-phrase to express it'.*

The issue of *vers libre* is only one aspect of the whole problem raised by the loss of 'the ideal'. And bewilderment and uncertainty are the natural reaction to the problem. The spectre which haunts poet and sociologist and historian alike is that what they are doing, in attending to 'things' or counting heads, or collating Elizabethan laundry-bills, may be a tautology.

* It is true that there is the same single metrical phrase or tune, something like the second half of a Latin hexameter, haunting most of the verse of the *Cantos*, but Pound does not use it as a norm from which to diverge but rather as a pattern towards which to converge.

It seems to require some jump into religion or mysticism to lay this spectre. You need some faith in a pre-existing harmony between words and reality—something like Pound's belief in 'permanent metaphor' or Williams's belief in the 'grain' of things—so that the responsibility for breaking silence can be lain on the world as much as on the writer. Whether the writer is an emptied vessel or a bristling bush, it is the world which makes the first step to fill him or brush against his spines. Short of some such belief, all you seem to have left, as an argument for writing, is Samuel Beckett's uncomfortable one: that the writer is someone who *can't stop* talking, though knowing there is nothing to say.

The need to come to terms with the fear that there is nothing to say, more than that, simply, 'there was *this*, against a background of nothingness', is beautifully defined in Thom Gunn's poems. These scrupulous, philosophical poems are the clearest statement there has been in verse of an anti-dualistic 'world-picture': a picture of discrete entities revolving with 'disinterested hard energy' against a void—or what is worse than a void, a flux of 'purposeless matter'. The key notions are outline, the skin or black leather, and self-enclosure, like that of the 'autonomous' work of art of the Symbolists. So the old man in Gunn's 'Taylor Street',

> . . . his big crumpled
> body anxiously cupped
> by himself, in himself, as
> he leans over himself . . .

His characters make

> . . . the large gesture of solitary man,
> Resisting, by embracing, nothingness.

And when the defensive outline is momentarily breached, by touch, the most 'blind' of the senses, what results is not a relationship with an individual but a merging with everybody:

> . . . the place is
> not found but seeps
> from our touch in
> continuous creation, dark
> enclosing cocoon round

ourselves alone, dark
wide realm where we
walk with everyone.
('Touch')

I bring in Thom Gunn for his clarity rather than for any peculiar artistic modernity. He puts the influence of William Carlos Williams to brilliant use in the lines I have quoted, but Williams is only one influence among many for him; he strikes me as an eclectic poet. Still, by whatever means, his poems catch very faithfully that fear that the whole act of writing may be a tautology—all the pretensions of writing having been reduced to a mere pointing.

However, a theory of art has been put forward recently which, by taking anti-dualism one step further, seems to take the sting out of this fear. This is the line developed by, among others, Susan Sontag in *Against Interpretation* (1967). And at first sight the theory also seems to offer a way round the stark choice between Symbolist and Bauhaus theory—between the desperate unity of the autonomous work of art, outlined against a void, or the utopian unity attainable by breaking down the barriers between art and life and so ultimately abolishing art. What the theory says is that it is time we gave up the old dualistic opposition of form to content in art. What is needed is not merely to restate the form-content relationship in a subtler way, but to give up talking about 'content' altogether. For a work of art is an object, among other objects—a piece of 'pure, untranslatable, sensuous immediacy'—and it only does harm to speak of it in terms of divisions and distinctions. And having given up the notion of 'content', we must automatically give up 'interpretation', since the whole purpose of interpretation is to prize out the 'content' from works of art (the 'real' or 'latent', as opposed to the 'manifest', content). And it is time we did give it up, the argument goes. For interpretation is an 'impious' activity, one which has sometimes been useful in the past, as a means of explaining away sanctified but inconvenient texts, but which in our present situation is 'reactionary, impertinent, cowardly, stifling'. Works of art, including literary ones, do not have a 'meaning'. They are what they are, and the job of the critic is simply to describe them, as if they were a rock or a flower.

This appears at first sight to get the best of both worlds:

the 'autonomousness' of works of art without the desperation, and the egalitarianism of the Bauhaus without the utopianism. But, in fact, though it avoids the revolutionary utopianism of the Bauhaus, it is still intensely utopian, and entails the breaking-down of barriers between 'high' culture and 'pop' culture, between the unique and the mass-produced and finally between art and life. And by throwing, not this time the poet but the critic, out of the Republic, and with him the tension between criticism and creation within the artist himself, it aims at a negative utopia, from which value is banished.

None the less, I don't think that the only answer to the fear that writing may be a tautology is a leap into religion or mysticism. In losing the sense of 'the ideal', and with it our whole unspoken confidence in referring things to a frame or measure, we have lost a great prop; indeed it takes some realising just how great. But we mustn't exaggerate. We have lost a deep-seated instinct, but it doesn't mean we are left helpless, deprived of all power to construct systems of value, or to use the words which imply them. For instance, it still makes sense to talk of people's *reputations*, and we don't have to resort to talk about their 'public image' instead,* even though we no longer think of reputations as ratified by eternal laurels. It still makes sense to elaborate systems of right conduct and manners, even though we harbour no Platonic archetypes of social order. And it still makes sense to create literature. For, just as the final justification for literary criticism is that you can't stop yourself from criticising, any more than you can stop breathing, so you cannot stop producing systems of value—they are, as Sartre says, what all along your life reveals you to have been making, whether consciously or not. And as art is a matter of giving permanence to apprehended values, then—no reason not to write. There is a humanist justification for writing, if you prefer it, as I think you should if you have a choice, to a mystical or religious one. Though as to the form that writing will take from now on, certain trends do seem to be indicated and certain avenues to be now closed: it looks as though metaphor might be going to take a less central place in literature, and writers to be going to be less keen, or less able, to create sustained fictions.

---

* See pp. 141–8.

I began this book by asking how it could be right to use the word 'image' as a synonym for 'metaphor', since an image, in the ordinary sense of the word, is a quite different thing from a comparison. And I tried to argue that this was not just an idle preference in the choice of words: for the terms 'image' and 'imagery' in their current sense (and the related term 'world') were bad ones, charged with all the paradoxes about works of art but none of their nature. But then I asked what were the philosophical reasons and historical causes why critics should want to use the words in this way, collapsing something double into something single. And the more I looked at them, the stronger they seemed. However, the fact that dualisms have so properly come under suspicion, and that it has become necessary to suspect every duality of being a worn-out fiction, does not mean that every one must be; though on the other hand, it provides an excellent reason why, as in the case of the word 'metaphor', people should assume that it is, in the teeth of all evidence.

But then, we need not think of metaphor as a lonely exception. There is an irreducible dualism in all art, but to a peculiar degree in the literature, in the fact that a work has to be recreated or 'realised' as an imaginative object by the reader or spectator. This is not the 'effect' of the work on the spectator, it is its whole existence—its only means of existence. And it is through this duality in the way a work of art exists that human value comes to be involved in art at all.

APPENDIX: THE PUBLIC IMAGE

It would be nice to be able to release the word 'image' from its inverted commas at last, but one more aspect of it needs looking at first. For the word 'image' has set up a whole new line of business in the last ten or fifteen years in its sense of 'public image', and this throws an interesting sidelight on its literary use. 'Psychiatric Nurses Seek a New Image'; 'Polishing the British Image in Australia': the term for which 'image' is a substitute here is 'reputation'. And in 'reputation' we have, *par excellence*, a word which involves notions of preconceived standards and criteria. It is likewise a word which smells vaguely of metaphysics. And when people have recently exorcised from their vocabularies the ghosts of so many useless metaphysical entities, it is natural for them to suspect metaphysics even in harmless and necessary words. 'Reputation' is particularly vulnerable. For it doesn't denote merely an abstract category, like 'honour' or 'justice'; it seems to refer to something which actually exists or might exist. A man *has* a reputation: and if he has a good reputation, we feel it to be more than mere opinion to say that he has added to it, or lost part of it. We feel it to be, within limits, a verifiable fact.

The word 'image' comes in very conveniently here, as a substitute. For whereas 'reputation', being an immaterial catogery, seems to be stepping outside its province in denoting a thing such as might actually exist, 'image' is fairly and squarely a word which refers to the existing world. An 'image', for this purpose at least, is a thing, a thing in the sense in which a reflection in a mirror is a thing—or if you prefer it, a phenomenon. (It is not to the purpose that you can't say exactly *where* it exists.)

The difference which it makes, though, if you substitute the word 'image' for 'reputation', is very large. For, to begin with, a 'public image', as people conceive of it, is something (a reflex) which can be implanted in the mind directly—whereas you cannot directly alter your own reputation: you can only behave rightly and wait for your reward. Again, to have a 'reputation' implies that other people are actively making some kind of assessment of you, whereas 'public image' merely implies that people passively acquire certain associations, or conditioned reflexes to, your name. Then, a 'reputation' implies that there are two things involved: observable behaviour, and a judgement passed upon it, which may subsequently be modified. To speak of a 'public image', on the other hand, implies that there is either nothing, or something unknown and altogether different, behind the image, so that there cannot be any interplay between the man and his 'image'. A 'reputation' also implies a balance of praise against censure, perhaps quite a complex balance; whereas a 'public image' is a whole, only replaceable (as in the case of mental *spectra*, or images in the literal sense) by another whole or 'image'. Hence a 'public image' must always be a poor and thin affair, something without the dense texture of reality.

The classic discussion of this use of the word 'image' is Daniel Boorstin's *The Image*. For him, the word is a degenerate substitute for the word 'ideal' and a moral counterpart to the pseudo-event (his name for synthetic events, or 'self-fulfilling prophecies', fabricated by the public relations industry in order that they can be reported). 'What the pseudo-event is in the world of fact,' he says, 'the image is in the world of value. The image is a pseudo-ideal.' His book is a wholesale indictment of modern Western (and especially American) society for having jettisoned 'ideals' in favour of 'images'.

> Now the language of images is everywhere. Everywhere it has displaced the language of ideals. If the right 'image' will elect a President or sell an automobile, a religion, a cigarette, or a suit of clothes, why can it not make America herself—or the American Way of Life—a saleable commodity all over the earth?[1]

And he defines the difference between 'ideal-thinking' and 'image-thinking' as follows:

> An ideal . . . contrasted to an image, is not synthetic. When we think of an ideal, we think of something already there. It was created by tradition, by history, or by

God. It is perfect, but it is not simplified. It is not ambiguous (or ambiguous only in a very different sense). Its implications are not passive. An ideal is what we actively strive towards, not what we fit into. Credibility is irrelevant. Charity, justice, equality, mercy, are no less ideals because no man or society ever lived up to them. Ideals are needed *because* in their perfect form, they are somehow hard to believe.

An image is something *we* have a claim on. It must serve our purposes. Images are means. If a corporation's image of itself or a man's image of himself is not useful, it is discarded. Another may fit better. The image is made to order, tailored to us. An ideal, on the other hand, has a a claim on us. It does not serve us; we serve it. If we have trouble striving towards it, we assume the matter is with us, and not with the ideal.[2]

Boorstin's is a valuable and cogent book, but I think there are weaknesses in it. He talks too apocalyptically; and this comes, I think, from taking the word 'image' too much on trust. In dealing with the term, as perhaps now I have succeeded in showing, one always needs to have a sense for what a strange word it is, and how many ambiguities and concealed metaphors, and metaphors-within-metaphors, lurk within it. Of course, he is concerned not so much with what people mean by the word as why they should want to use it. And, obviously, he would allow that often they don't mean much at all. Clearly, a 'public image' must be a pretty cloudy sort of entity if so many qualities can be attributed to it, or so many operations can be applied to it—if it can be 'cohesive', or 'open-ended'; if you can 'build' a 'public image', and 'bolster' it, 'air' it, 'impair' it, 'synthesise' it, 'doctor' it, 'repair' it, 'refurbish' it. We are not being told much when we read that 'The Home Secretary yesterday painted a new image of the prison officer', or 'Mr. Kisch talks learnedly about the image of the Eden hat'. Indeed, there's a lot of clean fun to be had in this vein from Boorstin's own book. I liked it particularly when the London correspondent of the *New York Times* explained to his readers, at the time of Dr. Fisher's retirement as Archbishop of Canterbury, that he had 'served as the chief "image" of the Anglican Church for sixteen years'. Popery indeed. And though there tends to be a nasty flavour to the word in the sense of 'public image', a totally baseless pretension to sociological insight, it is not worth worrying too much, from a social point of view, about the word itself. Words like 'image' have a vogue, simply for their mystery-value. And, at least in advertising and public relations, the word does have a real function, and the millions of dollars spent on manipulating the 'image' of a product or a politician are not being squandered on a fantasy. However, the very fact that so many verbs and epithets can be applied to an 'image'—that, apparently, almost any sort of metaphor can be used of it—is a clue to what lies behind the use of the word.

The point is that 'image' in this sense is close to 'image' in the sense of 'mental image'—closer than you might think at first sight. As I've said earlier, one tends to think of a mental image (i.e. the imitation of an actual visual experience) as a definite and identifiable phenomenon, occurring in a definite place and time (even if one can't quite say where, exactly). This, however, is an illusion. No physical event is taking place when you form a mental image, only a 'make-believe', and hence a mental image is a much less definite affair than one tends to assume—indeed there is no clear dividing line between mental images and 'thoughts'. A mental image 'means' to you more or less what you want it to mean—it stands in a largely symbolic relation to the actual experience of seeing the thing in question—it's a useful peg to hang your thought on, as a carved image of the Virgin is a useful peg on which to hang thoughts of the mother of God. In itself, it's almost as loose, as sketchy and fleeting a thing, as little a definite 'thing' indeed, as what people mean by a 'public image'.

Now, an essential feature of mental images is their automatic quality. For most of us when we read a word like 'hippopotamus', or a name like 'President Nixon', a picture comes up into our mind automatically. We *can't help* its doing so. The picture may not be at all helpful to us, and if we want to go on thinking about the subject, we will abandon the first 'image' for more useful ones. This initial automatic 'picturing' represents only the small change of our mind: not the sum of our real knowledge of hippopotamuses or of President Nixon, only the loose cash of our stock responses. And in this, as indeed in most ways, it is very much the same sort of thing as is meant by the 'public image'. What is real about this business of the 'public image' is the fact of human automatism. Advertisers and public relations experts, when they work on the 'image' of a product (or a personality or an institution), are not attempting something so impracticable as implanting a particular 'picture' of the product in people's minds. What they are implanting is a reflex. They are conditioning the consumer, by some system of potential pains and rewards, and according to known behaviouristic methods, to choose one brand of goods rather than another when the occasion arises. The actual nature of the 'picture' or 'image' the consumer forms is irrelevant. (Indeed, as behaviourist psychology tells us, *all* speculations about what goes on in the 'mind' of the subject are unnecessary; all that needs be studied is his observable behaviour.) That is why the word 'image' tends to be misleading. And of course the fact that advertisers (as opposed to public relations men) do most of their work through pictures in the literal sense (posters, and so on) is not to the point. What counts is the conditioning of the consumer so that when he is faced with having to choose, say, a brand of tobacco, he allows himself to be prompted—for lack of any objective criterion of choice—by an implanted irrational association.

Boorstin goes wrong, therefore, in treating 'image-thinking' as a question of belief. His charge against 'image-thinking' is that it means surrendering to illusions. 'It is not only advertising which has become a tissue of contrivance and illusions,' he says. 'Rather, it is the whole world.' But, in fact, I don't think this is a modern trend. People, if anything, are rather more cynical and sceptical than they used to be. The romantic novelettes of fifty years ago are more innocent than anything we have now, and so are the films of Hollywood's heyday; and television plays, as we know, have to be studiously everyday and documentary in their flavour. You can only get away with horror and fantasy on television on the tacit understanding that you are 'sending them up'. And Boorstin himself mentions, that one of the favourite devices of advertisers is to take the consumer behind the scenes, flattering his sense of himself as unfooled and in the know.

> . . . some of the most effective advertising nowadays
> consists of circumstantial descriptions of how the advertising
> images were contrived; how tests were devised, how
> tradesmarks were designed, and how the corporate cosmetics

were applied. . . . Paradoxically . . . the more we know about the tricks of image-building, about the calculation, ingenuity, and effort that have gone into a particular image, the more satisfaction we have from the image itself. The elaborate contrivance proves to us that we are really justified (and not stupid either) in being taken in.[3]

Of course, there is illusion in believing yourself to be without illusions. But what experts in the manipulation of 'public images' are mainly exploiting is not beliefs or illusions but conditioned reflexes—i.e. automatism. (Behaviourist techniques do not depend on belief. A patient undergoing aversion-therapy does not have to believe the electric shocks are 'punishing' him for having unacceptable desires.) These experts succeed in making people buy one brand of cigarettes or detergent rather than another not by giving them a belief or illusions about it, but by inducing them to act automatically in the situation of choice. It is a perfectly real power they are exploiting, one which works best in cases either where (as with detergents) there is no real difference between the alternatives the customer has to choose from, or where (as is the case, for most voters, in elections) he has no first-hand way of discovering the difference. The 'image' (whatever you mean by that) which the purchaser or voter forms of what he chooses is not an active factor in the whole business—it is merely a by-product of his acting, or reacting, in a certain way.—This is a good example of how the word 'image' always tends to crumble under scrutiny.

Hence, I think Boorstin, in contrasting 'ideal-thinking' with 'image-thinking', has somehow got hold of the wrong antithesis. There is a much more clear-cut contrast to be made, and that is between 'image' and 'reputation'. 'Manipulating images', or what goes under that name (I would prefer to call it 'Pavlovian advertising') is always concerned with situations of ignorance. As most of us are ignorant most of the time, that opens a wide field of action. And if you *are* in a state of ignorance—if you have got to choose between two almost indistinguishable products or between two personalities on whom you have not much chance of making a first-hand judgement—there is nothing intrinsically silly in letting irrational factors sway you. Even a bad reason may be better than no reason. I'm not trying to defend Pavlovian advertising, which is certainly a pernicious thing; all I mean is that to be a willing victim of it is not the sin that Boorstin makes out.

For it's not as if thinking in terms of 'images' could really displace thinking in terms of 'reputations'. Not all public situations are situations of ignorance. There are plenty, for instance, in which one has first-hand knowledge of *people.* And one only has to have worked in an office to know that, within such a context, reputation-making still goes on in the way it has always done. Round each member of an office staff or the staff of any institution, an elaborate invisible structure of reputation is rapidly built up—really a structure of expectation, representing the residue of successive communal judgements on his past actions. It is like a living organism, all the time imperceptibly growing and changing, and liable to occasional dramatic transformations—when the subject suddenly reveals a new trait, or makes a conspicuous triumph or false step—but with a continuity and permanence about it also. Within that institution, though increasingly only there, the reputation is solid, and cannot disappear or change unrecognisably overnight. It is something quite unlike an 'image', being much richer than any 'image' can be, encapsulating a complex reality and not merely standing as a cypher for it, as an 'image' does.

'Reputation' is still an indispensable concept, wherever people are brought together at close quarters. And the fact that they are sometimes genuinely shy of the word at the moment, and prefer to use the word 'image', does not really indicate the moral degeneration that Boorstin imagines. It is more the result of a very reasonable fear (though one that happens to be unjustified in this case) of using 'metaphysical' language.—At the same time, I think it's a pity. It does seem as if, not only this word, but other innocent and valuable conceptual words of the same kind, were in danger. It's something of this sort that Iris Murdoch had in mind, as a cause of decay in the recent novel, when she wrote:

> What have we lost here? And what have we perhaps never had? We have suffered a general loss of concepts, the loss of a moral and political vocabulary. We no longer use a spread-out substantial picture of the manifold virtues of man and society.[4]

One more point is worth making. When Boorstin talks about 'an ideal' or 'ideals', contrasting these with 'images', he plainly means something rather different from what I meant earlier by 'the ideal'. He speaks of an 'ideal' as something we 'pursue' or 'actively strive towards'. Whereas in the sense I wanted to give the word (the sense for which I took the frame as a symbol) there is no question of pursuing or attaining the ideal—not even of an endless pursuit of it like that of Browning's Grammarian. It is a quite static, and even intimate, relationship between a human phenomenon and an order of things in which it can have no part. Boorstin's is the nineteenth-century conception, according to which a man 'has' ideals—they are 'his', just as other men have others—and it has a flavour of the very 'image-thinking' which he is attacking.

NOTES

CHAPTER 1

1 Caroline Spurgeon: *Shakespeare's Imagery and What It Tells Us*, 1935, pp. 8–9.
2 Ibid.
3 Burke: *On the Sublime and the Beautiful*, Part V, Section 5.
4 Ibid.
5 Berkeley: *Principles of Human Knowledge*, Introduction, §.13.
6 A. D. Nuttall: *Two Concepts of Allegory*, 1967, p. 63.
7 Ibid., p. 79.
8 William Empson: 'Argufying in Poetry', a Third Programme talk reprinted in *The Listener*, 22 August 1963.
9 Ibid.
10 Diderot: *Lettre sur les aveugles* (ed R. Nicklaus), 1951, p. 16 (present author's translation).

CHAPTER 2

1 Puttenham: *The Arte of English Poesie*, 1589, fol. 204.
2 Wilson: *Arte of Rhetorique*, 1562, fol. 106, verso.
3 Nathan Bailey: *Universal Etymological English Dictionary*, 1731.
4 Ibid.
5 R. Frazer: 'The origin of the word "image" ', in *Eng. Lit. Hist.* vol. xxvii, pp. 149–61.
6 Ibid.
7 Dennis: Preface to *The Passion of Byblis: Critical Works* (ed. Hooker) 1939–43, vol. 1 and 2.
8 Lord Kames: *Elements of Criticism*, 4 edn., 1769, vol. 1, p. 93.
9 N. Rowe: 'Some account of the life of Mr. William Shakespeare', in *The Works of . . . Shakespeare*, 1709, p. xxii.
10 Conversations recorded by Christopher Wordsworth in *Memoirs of William Wordsworth*, 1851, vol. 2, p. 477.
11 W. B. Yeats: *Essays and Introductions*, 1961, pp. 46–7.
12 Ibid., pp. 156–7.

(2)

13 D. Davie: *Ezra Pound: Poet and Sculptor*, 1965, p. 73.
14 R. de Gourmont: *Le Problème du style*, 3 edn., 1902, pp. 86–7. (Present author's translation.)
15 Ibid., p. 91
16 Ibid., p. 90.
17 Ibid., p. 101.

(3)

18 Ezra Pound: 'Vorticism', in *Gaudier-Brzeska*, 1916, p. 109 fn.
19 Ibid., pp. 146–7.
20 Ibid., p. 103.
21 Ezra Pound: *Literary Essays*, 1954, p. 154.
22 C. K. Stead: *The New Poetic*, 1964, p. 103.
23 Ezra Pound: *Letters* (ed. D. D. Paige), 1951, p. 285.
24 Ibid., p. 154.
25 D. Davie: *Articulate Energy*, 1955, p. 125.

CHAPTER 3

1 M. A. Rugoff: *Donne's Imagery: A Study in Creative Sources*, 1939, pp. 13–14.
2 Ibid., pp. 14–15.
3 Ibid., p. 16.
4 R. Heilman: *Magic in the Web*, Lexington, 1956, p. 239.
5 P. Haeffner: *A Critical Commentary on Shakespeare's 'Richard III'*, 1963, pp. 52–3.
6 W. Clemen: *The Development of Shakespeare's Imagery*, 1951, pp. 82–3.
7 Ibid., pp. 99–100.
8 Ibid., p. 213.
9 Ibid., pp. 227–8.
10 R. Tuve: *Elizabethan and Metaphysical Imagery*, 1947, p. 49.
11 Ibid., p. 79.
12 Ibid., pp. 275–6.
13 Ibid., pp. 43–4.
14 Ibid., pp. 43–4.
15 C. Day Lewis: *The Poetic Image*, 1947, p. 18.
16 M. Murry: 'Metaphor', in *John Clare and Other Studies*, 1950, p. 85.
17 Ibid., p. 87.
18 H. Kenner: *The Art of Poetry*, New York, 1959, pp. 47–8.
19 Ibid., p. 37.
20 Ibid., p. 48.

21 F. R. Leavis: 'Imagery and movement: Notes in the analysis of Poetry', *Scrutiny*, September 1945, p. 124.
22 Ibid., p. 119.
23 F. R. Leavis: *Revaluation*, 1936, p. 55.
24 F. R. Leavis: 'Imagery and movement', etc., p. 120.
25 Ibid.

CHAPTER 4

1 R. Frazer: 'The origin of the word "image" ', in *Eng. Lit. Hist.* vol. xxvii, pp. 149–61.
2 Fenollosa: in *The Chinese Written Character as a Medium for Poetry* (ed. Ezra Pound), 1936.
3 Ibid., p. 26.
4 T. E. Hulme: *Speculations*, 1924, p. 134.
5 Jonathan Swift: *Gulliver's Travels*, Book III, Chapter 6.
6 D. Davie: *Articulate Energy*, 1955, p. 108.
7 S. Mallarmé: Preface to Réné Ghil's *Traité du verbe.*
8 William Carlos Williams: *Selected Essays*, 1954, p. 340.
9 R. Kostelanetz: 'Marshal McLuhan', reprinted in *Innovations* (ed. B. Bergonzi), 1968, p. 144.
10 W. K. Wimsatt: *The Verbal Icon*, pp. 115-16.
11 Quoted by Henry Treece in *Dylan Thomas*, 1949, p. 47, note 1.

CHAPTER 5

1 See F. Yates: *The Art of Memory*, 1968, p. 253.
2 Ibid., p. 286.
3 Ibid., p. 253.
4 Ibid., *passim.*
5 R. W. Short: 'Henry James's World of Images', in *PMLA*, 1953
6 Josephine Miles: 'The problem of imagery', *Sewanee Review*, lviii, 1950, p. 523.
7 R. W. Short: op. cit., p. 948.
8 M. Proust: *Swann's Way*, pp. 183–4.
9 M. Proust: *Time Regained*, p. 412.
10 F. Kermode: *London Magazine*, November 1958, p. 24.
11 Henry James: Preface to *The Awkward Age.*
12 T. S. Eliot: *The Sacred Wood*, 1920.
13 W. J. Harvey: *Character and the Novel*, 1965, p. 34.
14 Charles Burkhart: *I. Compton-Burnett*, 1965.

CHAPTER 6

1 John Ruskin: *Modern Painters*, Part III. Section I, Chapter 13.
2 Ibid.

3 F. Fénéon, quoted by J. Rewald in *Georges Seurat*, New York 1946, p. 65.
4 E. W. Said: 'Merleau-Ponty', in *Kenyon Review*, January 1967.
5 W. Gropius: *Bauhaus*, 1923. (Translated by Bayer as *The Theory and Organization of the Bauhaus*.)
6 H. Kenner: *The Poetry of Ezra Pound*, 1951, pp. 102–5, *passim*.

APPENDIX

1 Daniel J. Boorstin: *The Image*, 1962, p. 183.
2 Ibid.
3 Ibid., p. 109.
4 Iris Murdoch: 'Against Dryness', in *Encounter*, January 1961.

INDEX

INDEX